All five men froze, ~~_____~~er, the other three at John Locke. Cooper looked at the handful of gold Cal Nieves had.

"There's a lot of gold here," Del said to Locke and Cooper. "Plenty for all of us."

The look in all of their eyes was unmistakable to Locke.

"Don't do it, boy," Cooper said.

Cal went for his gun, too impatient for Del to call the play. Locke moved the muzzle of his rifle a fraction of an inch and shot him dead. Cal was thrown from the buckboard. Clete Cloninger went for his weapon, and Cooper fired, hitting Cloninger and driving him off his horse to the ground.

"Don't—" Malcolm Turner said, but Cooper fired again and took him from his saddle. That left Del Morgan and Red Sinclair, both of whom were scrambling for their weapons. Morgan, never a hand with a gun, had his go flying from his grip even before Cooper's bullet struck him. Sinclair was such a huge target that both Locke and Cooper put a bullet in him. The big man sat his saddle for a few moments, looking puzzled, before he slumped and fell to the ground.

Locke walked over to all the bodies, checked them, then turned to Cooper. "They're all dead."

"Their choice," the ex-marshal said, thumbing fresh rounds into his rifle. . . .

THE WIDOWMAKER

BOOK TWO

TURNBACK CREEK

ROBERT J. RANDISI

POCKET STAR BOOKS

New York London Toronto Sydney

This book is a work of fiction. Names, characters, places and incidents are products of the author's imagination or are used fictitiously. Any resemblance to actual events or locales or persons, living or dead, is entirely coincidental.

An *Original* Publication of POCKET BOOKS

 A Pocket Star Book published by
POCKET BOOKS, a division of Simon & Schuster, Inc.
1230 Avenue of the Americas, New York, NY 10020

Copyright © 2004 by Robert J. Randisi

ISBN: 0-7434-7680-8

First Pocket Books printing September 2004

10 9 8 7 6 5 4 3 2 1

POCKET STAR BOOKS and colophon are registered trademarks of Simon & Schuster, Inc.

Cover art: Deel

Manufactured in the United States of America

For information regarding special discounts for bulk purchases, please contact Simon & Schuster Special Sales at 1-800-456-6798 or business@simonandschuster.com

To my courageous friend, Ed Gorman

THE
WIDOWMAKER
BOOK TWO
TURNBACK CREEK

PROLOGUE

Dan Hagen stared down into the Devil's Basin. It was as if God's hand had come down and scooped out a section of the mountain. When it rained, the section filled with water very quickly. Hagen knew of six people who had been caught during storms and drowned there. Since that time, the basin had become off-limits to anyone with knowledge of the mountain. No one had more knowledge of this mountain than Danny Hagen. He'd been traveling over it for more than fifty of his seventy years. In fact, some folks even referred to it as Hagen's Mountain.

"There it is, Henrietta," he said, speaking to his mule. "The Devil's Basin. Quickest way over the mountain and the most dangerous at this time of the year."

Hagen took off his battered hat and looked up at the darkening sky. Rain was coming. It would be light at first, showers good only for making traveling messy. The rocks would get wet and slippery. Lower down, the dirt would turn to mud. Water would run off the mountain into

Turnback Creek—both the town and the creek itself.

Hagen knew he had time to traverse the basin before the storms became so heavy that it filled with water. He had time to get over the mountain and move on. When the time came and the storms and water receded, he would return to his mountain, crossing over once again at the Devil's Basin.

But, for now, it was time to move on.

"Come on, Henrietta," he said, putting his hat back on and pulling on her lead. "Into the basin."

The mule refused to move.

"Now, now," Hagen said. "Ain't no time to be stubborn, ol' girl. We gotta go."

Still, the mule didn't move.

"I know you don't like this, girl," Hagen said. "I don't, either, but it's the shortest way."

Actually, he did like it. He liked knowing the mountain well enough to know when the basin could or could not be traversed. He thought he was the only man who did know that.

"Come on, girl," he said, shaking her lead. "Time to go."

This time, the mule did move, and the shaggy-looking animal and the disheveled-looking man started into the Devil's Basin.

The sky continued to darken, and eventually the misty rain started falling. It was the kind of rain that just lay over everything—rocks, ground, animals, men—making it all wet and, before you knew it, soaking wet. But it didn't roll off the mountain and into the basin.

Not just yet.

ONE

Ellsworth, Kansas
1877

John Locke looked out the window of his hotel room and saw his friend, Marshal Dale Cooper, standing in the street—alone. Cooper hesitated in front of his office, took a deep breath, adjusted his gun belt, and then stepped into the street.

"This is not going to happen," Locke said.

He turned, grabbed his gun belt from the bedpost, and left the room, still strapping it on. He wanted to get down to the street before Cooper could get very far.

As he came out the front door, almost at a run, he saw his friend walking down the street with a purposeful stride.

"Coop!"

He hit the street running and caught up to his friend, who turned to look at him as Locke grabbed his arm. His jaw was set, and his eyes were steely. He looked grim.

"John," Cooper said. "What are you doing here?"

"Same thing you are."

"I'm wearin' a badge," Cooper said. "I have to be here. It's my job. You don't."

"I'm not letting you do this alone, Coop," Locke said. "It's as simple as that."

Cooper stared at his friend, then took a deputy's badge from his pocket and held it out.

"No," Locke said, holding up his hand. "Let's just do it."

Cooper put the badge away and shook his head. "I'm gettin' too old for this, John."

"You're not even fifty yet."

"I'm forty-eight."

"See?"

"Forty-eight seem a good age to die to you?"

"I'm forty-one, Dale," Locke said, "and that doesn't seem a good age to die."

"At the other end of this street are going to be five cowboys," Cooper said. "They're all going to be wearing guns. Do you know what that means?"

"Yes," Locke said. "It means they're cowboys wearing guns when they're more used to holding a lariat. It means that when we reach them, they will officially be outnumbered."

Cooper thought that over, then nodded and said, "That's one way of looking at it."

Locke slapped the lawman on the back and said, "That's the only way to look at it, my friend."

* * *

Turnback Creek, Montana

As John Locke rode into the mining town of Turnback Creek, Montana, he realized it had been more than ten years since he had last seen Dale Cooper. That debacle in Ellsworth with the cowboys. It had cost Cooper his job as marshal, and after that, Locke had pretty much lost track of his friend. If he'd taken to wearing a badge somewhere else, Locke had never heard about it. Then, out of the blue, last week Locke received a telegram in Las Vegas, New Mexico, from Cooper, asking him to meet him in Turnback Creek. Their friendship was such that, even after all the years of silence, Locke left immediately.

The town looked fairly typical—ramshackle buildings, badly rutted streets filled with water after several days of unrelenting rain. It was falling now, the rain, in a misty drizzle. Locke's shirt and jeans were soaked, his leather vest wet. He wanted some dry clothes and a hot meal even before he tried to find Dale Cooper.

The telegram had been cryptic, just a line asking Locke to meet him. Didn't say where he was staying or where to find him. But locating Cooper was going to have to wait until he got situated and dry.

He came to a hotel before he came to a livery, so he stopped to get a room.

"Do you know a man named Cooper?" he asked the clerk as he signed the register. "Dale Cooper?"

"Dale Cooper?" the young man repeated thoughtfully. "Can't say I do, sir."

Before returning the register book to the clerk, Locke

checked the last few pages to see if Cooper had checked in and the clerk simply had forgotten the name. Not only had he not, but no one had.

"Room five," the clerk said. "Top of the stairs and turn right. Do you have a bag?"

"I'm going to take my horse to the livery stable," Locke said, accepting the key. "I'll look at the room when I come back. No, no bag. I'll just have my saddlebags."

"Yes, sir."

Locke turned to leave, then turned back.

"Not a very busy time here, is it?"

"It never is, sir," the clerk said. "All we have is the mine, and most of the miners live elsewhere. Right now, there's only two other people staying in the hotel."

"Okay," Locke said. "Now, if you'll just tell me where the livery stable is, I'd be obliged."

Following the clerk's directions, Locke rode to the livery stable and left his horse in the care of an old man he suspected got along better with horses than with men. He got little more than a grunt from the man but felt confident leaving his animal with him.

He walked back to the hotel, carrying his rifle and saddlebags, looking the town over along the way. It was quiet and probably would stay that way until the miners got off work and started hitting the saloons.

"Get your horse taken care of all right?" the clerk asked as he reentered the hotel.

"Just fine," Locke said.

"That's room five."

Locke showed the clerk the key. "I remember."

He went up the stairs, found his room, and let himself in. He locked the door behind him, tossed the saddlebags onto the bed, and leaned the rifle against the wall. The room was small but remarkably clean for a mining-town hotel. He'd stayed in much worse places in better towns.

He went to the window and looked down at the street. As he removed his wet shirt, he wondered where Dale Cooper was or if he was even in town yet—and what had he been doing for the past ten years?

He decided that his jeans weren't all that wet after all, especially since he was going to go back out into the drizzle. He took a clean shirt from his saddlebags and put it on, then used the wet one to wipe down his vest before donning that again as well. The black, flat-brimmed hat he wore was no worse the wear for the rain. He would have to clean his gun, though, when he came back to the room for the evening. For now, he removed it from his holster and wiped it down, too, with the shirt. He savored for a moment the way his fingers fit into the specially made grooves in the handle, then holstered it again, made sure it sat just right.

Before leaving the room, he utilized the wet, already dirty shirt for one last task, to wipe down his rifle, which he left behind as he went in search of a nice, hot meal.

Once again, it was directions from the clerk that got him where he wanted to go. It was a small café several blocks from the hotel, and as he approached, he could smell the cooking odors. Keeping to the boardwalk, he was able to avoid getting too wet again, which ensured that he'd be reasonably comfortable when he sat down to his meal.

He entered the café, which was small but had a homey feel to it. There was only one other table taken at the moment, by a man and a woman who didn't give him a second look.

"Can I help you?" a waiter asked.

"You can if that's coffee I smell."

"It is," the man said, "and good coffee, too."

"Then I'll take a table, a cup, and a thick steak."

"Sit anywhere you like, sir," the waiter said. "I'll fetch it for you right away."

"Thanks."

Locke sat away from the middle-aged couple and away from the front window. In a few moments, the waiter returned with not only a cup but a pot of coffee to go with it.

"You look like you been riding a while," he said, "so I brung you a whole pot."

"Thanks," Locke said.

He poured himself a cup of coffee and stole a glance at the couple. They seemed intent on their meal and weren't talking to each other. The man looked to be in his early fifties, but the woman was younger than he'd first thought when he'd pegged them as a middle-aged couple. She appeared to be in her mid-thirties, a handsome woman with pale skin and long dark hair worn behind her head in a bun.

When the waiter came out with a steak dinner, Locke lost interest in the couple and applied himself to the hunk of beef and the steaming vegetables. He hadn't eaten this well in quite a while, and he became thoroughly engrossed in the meal. He was finishing up when the couple called for their check, paid it, and stood up to leave. He was surprised when the woman stopped and spoke to him as they passed his table. The man stopped with her, stood just behind her right shoulder.

"I haven't seen a man eat quite that fast in a long time," she said, gracing him with a smile that transformed her from merely handsome to quite beautiful.

"It's been a while since I had a meal this good, ma'am," he said. "I hope my eating habits didn't offend you."

"Molly . . ." the man with her said.

"Wait for me outside, George," she said.

The man looked as if he wanted to say something else, but he abruptly turned and left. Locke wondered if they were married or if the man merely worked for her. Either situation could have explained the couple's apparent relationship.

"I wasn't offended at all," she said, continuing from where they'd left off. Locke wondered what he'd done to invite this attention. As attractive as she was, there was still some food on his plate that he wanted to get to before it cooled off.

"In fact, it's nice to meet a man with an appetite, and manners," she said. ""Do you mind if I sit a moment?""

Surprised again, he said, "Go ahead."

"Thank you." She sat opposite him. He could see the man waiting impatiently right outside the door.

"Have you just arrived in town?"

"Yes, ma'am."

"Well, I'm over at the Shillstone Mining office," she said. "You look like a man who might be looking for work. I need a man who's confident and knows what he's doing with a gun."

"What makes you think I'm that man?"

"Just a hunch." She leaned her elbows on the table and set her chin in her palm. "I usually go with my hunches."

"Well, I'm not looking for work, ma'am," Locke said, "but I'll keep that in mind."

"You do that, Mr. . . ."

"Locke," he said. "John Locke."

Her face froze for a moment, but then she smiled and said, "A pleasure to have met you, Mr. Locke."

"Ma'am."

As she went out the door and he returned to his food, the waiter came over with a fresh pot of coffee.

"That was Molly Shillstone," he said.

Locke looked up at the waiter.

"So I gathered."

"Owns the biggest mine hereabouts," the waiter said.

"You can leave the coffee," Locke said, not wanting any more interruptions, "and bring me some more vegetables."

"You want another hunk of beef with those vegetables?" the man asked. "Got it hot and ready."

Locke thought only a moment and said, "Hell, why not?"

TWO

Since the place was empty and the waiter had thrown the second hunk of beef in for free, Locke decided to go ahead and talk to the man. Well, actually, he let the man go ahead and talk to him, which he did from the seat right across from him.

"The gold played out a long time ago," the man said, "but Mrs. Shillstone's mine has a lot of other metals in it." His name was Felix, and on days like this, when it wasn't busy, he was both the cook and the waiter, but he wasn't the owner of the place. Locke had already gotten much more information about Felix than he wanted, but he didn't want to insult a man who very well might have been the only good cook in town.

"Like what other metals?" Locke asked.

"I'm not sure," Felix said, "but there's a lot of them, and a lot of uses for them."

Locke knew that some gold mines would also yield other ores, as well as some stones, such as diamonds.

"Any diamonds?"

"Diamonds?" Felix frowned. "I don't think so."

Locke pushed away the empty plate and poured himself another cup of coffee to wash both meals down. Actually, what he needed now was a cold beer, but he had a question or two for Felix before he left and went in search of a saloon.

"Felix, tell me, what did I do today to attract Mrs. Shillstone's attention?" he asked.

"Well," Felix said, "a couple of things. One, you're a stranger."

"What's that got to do with anything?"

"You ain't had time to take sides yet."

Locke was going to ask what sides, but he knew that in any town there were sides— usually two, sometimes more.

"What else?"

"You look like you can handle a gun."

"Why would she need someone who can handle a gun?"

"Payroll."

"What about it?"

"She's had one hit and doesn't want it to happen again."

"Someone robbed her payroll?"

Felix nodded.

"They hit it when it was on its way up the mountain," Felix said. "Her men ain't been paid in months, and they're about to quit on her."

"So she's got another payroll coming in?"

"Yep," Felix said. "End of the week, and she's gonna need somebody to deliver it up the mountain."

Locke sat back in his chair. "How much are we talking about?"

"Well, the first one was more than ten thousand dollars. Now, since the men ain't been paid in a while, they want more than they got comin', so this one figures to be about five times that."

"Fifty thousand dollars?"

"Maybe more."

"How do you know that?" Locke was wondering how a waiter knew so much about the woman's business.

"Hell, the whole town knows her business," Felix said. "After all, a lot of the businesses in town depend on the miners' havin' money to spend, and she's got the biggest mine and the most miners. Hell, it's everybody's business now, not just hers."

"So, with everybody knowing how much she's bringing in . . ."

". . . It's a sure bet this payroll's gonna be hit as well," Felix finished. "She needs somebody who can handle a gun to take it up there—and now she knows who you are."

Locke didn't rise to that bait.

"I mean . . . are you really John Locke . . . the Widowmaker?"

"I'm John Locke," he replied. "I don't know how many John Lockes there are, though."

"Well," Felix said, "if you're him—you, that is—she's definitely gonna want you to work for her. Probably pay you a pretty penny, too. If she loses another payroll, she's in lots of trouble—and so is this town."

"So, what'd you mean about taking sides?"

"She's not a well-liked woman, is all," Felix said. "There are them who feel the town could survive without her, but they ain't in the majority, I can tell you that."

"Well," Locke said, "it's too bad I'm not looking for a job. What do I owe you?"

"Seventy-five cents."

Locke gave the man a silver dollar and stood up.

"Who was that man with her?" Locke asked, out of curiosity. "She called him George."

"That's George Crowell."

"Husband?"

"No, he's her manager," Felix said. "Or foreman. I ain't sure what she calls him."

"Looks like she runs pretty rough-shod over him."

"That she does," Felix said, "and he lets her, because he's in love with her."

"And the whole town knows that, too?"

"Yup."

When they reached the door, Felix said, "Actually, Molly—that's Mrs. Shillstone, but everybody in town just calls her Molly—did hire somebody to take the payroll up the mountain."

"She did?" Locke asked. "Then why would she be looking to hire me to do the same thing?"

"Well . . ." Felix said. "She ain't all that sure she hired the right man for the job."

"And why's that?"

"Well . . . he's been sittin' around waitin' for the payroll to get to Kingdom Junction. Uh, that's where the railhead is."

"He's been waiting here or there?"

"Oh, here."

"So, what's wrong with that?" Locke asked. "What else has the man got to do but wait?"

"I think she's worried about where he's doin' his waitin'."

"And where's that?"

"The saloon."

"Drinking?"

"Oh, yeah," Felix said with a nod. "Supposed to be some big-time ex-lawman, too."

Locke stopped in his tracks, almost out the door.

"And what would his name be?"

"His name's Marshal Cooper," Felix said. "Dale Cooper. Ever heard of him?"

THREE

There were three saloons in Turnback Creek. According to Felix the waiter, Dale Cooper spent his days in the largest of the three. When he walked into the Three Aces Saloon, he spotted Cooper right away. He was sitting at a back table with his head down on it, one hand wrapped around a whiskey bottle. Locke decided not to approach his old friend right away, and instead went to the bar to get himself that beer. There were only three other men in the place, all of them standing at the bar.

"Beer," Locke said to the bartender, who was deep in conversation with two of the men.

"Comin' right up," the barman said, but he did not go for the beer right away.

"I'd like it now," Locke said.

The bartender, a young man in his thirties, turned his head and looked at Locke.

"I'll get it in a minute, old-timer," the man said. "I'm finishin' up a conversation here."

Locke reached across the bar and closed his left hand over the man's forearm.

"No," Locke said. "You're getting me a beer, and then you can go back to your conversation."

The bartender straightened up, and the two men he'd been talking to turned to face Locke, who stared back at the bartender while keeping the other two men in his peripheral vision.

It was a tense moment, and Locke wondered if they valued their conversation enough to go for their guns, but the decision was made for all of them by the other man in the room.

"Get him his beer, Al," the man said, "and stop being such an asshole."

The man was standing at the far end of the bar, and Al the bartender turned to look at him.

"Do it!" the man said wearily.

"Yeah, okay, Mike," the bartender said.

He drew a beer, and as he went to set the mug down, Locke said, "Don't spill it."

The man hesitated, then set the mug down gently and moved away to stand near his friends.

Locke lifted the beer and gestured to the man at the end of the bar, who lifted his own beer in return and then straightened up and started toward Locke. The badge on his chest was in plain view now, and as he reached Locke, the word *Sheriff* became clear.

"Much obliged, Sheriff," Locke said.

"John Locke, isn't it?" the man asked.

Locke hesitated long enough to study the man. He was forty or so, about six foot, heavy through the shoulders and chest, thick in the waist. Not a man to go hand-to-hand with. The gun on his hip was worn but cared for.

"Do I know you, Sheriff?"

"No," the lawman said, "but I know you. I saw you once, a few years ago—in Laramie, I think."

"I've been in Laramie."

Locke looked over at Cooper, who hadn't moved. He identified his friend from the bald spot on the crown of his head, which had spread but was still recognizable. It had been a sore spot with Cooper when he was in his forties. Apparently, now that he was almost sixty, it didn't matter much to him, for his hat was on the floor next to him.

"My name is Mike Hammet," the lawman said. "Been sheriff here about two years."

"Good for you."

"Not really," Hammet said, "but it's a job. And as part of my job, I've got to ask you what brings you to Turnback Creek."

Locke looked away from Cooper at the lawman.

"I'm here to meet someone."

"Who?"

"A friend."

"Anybody I'd know?"

"Maybe."

The lawman remained silent and waited. Locke gave him some credit for that.

"Dale Cooper."

Hammet looked over at the slumped man.

"Yeah, that's him," Locke said.

"I didn't know," Hammet said. "Marshal Dale Cooper."

"That's right."

"He's not wearin' a badge now."

"Apparently not."

"Friend of yours?"

"Yes," Locke said. "For a long time."

"He's not in very good shape," Hammet said. "Been here a few days, spends every day in here. What brought him here?"

"A job, I think."

"Workin' for who?" the lawman asked, then answered his own question. "Wait a minute . . . he ain't the one Molly Shillstone hired to transport her payroll, is he?"

"I don't know, Sheriff," Locke said. "I won't know what the job is until I talk to him."

"You'll have to wake him up first," Hammet said. "Sober him up. Either one might be hard to do."

"I guess."

Hammet's beer mug was almost empty. He set it down on the bar and said, "Good luck."

"Yeah," Locke said. "Thanks."

He carried his beer with him to Dale Cooper's table.

Sheriff Mike Hammet watched as Locke walked over to the table the older man was slumped on. He hadn't known he had a man with a reputation like Dale Cooper's in town, and now he had two men with reputations in Turnback Creek. He was going to have to keep an eye on them.

"Hey, Sheriff."

Hammet turned and looked at the bartender, whose voice was a whisper in his ear.

"What?"

"Is that really him?"

"Who?"

"The Widowmaker," Al said. "I'm askin' is that really John Locke the Widowmaker?"

"I guess it is," Hammet said.

"They say nobody knows which one the Widowmaker is," Al said, "him or the gun."

"So?"

"Do you know the answer?"

Hammet turned and looked at the bartender.

"What's it matter, Al?" he asked. "Either way, you're just as dead, ain't you?"

The bartender was thinking about that as the sheriff walked out the door.

FOUR

Locke walked to the table, put his beer down, and sat across from Dale Cooper. This close, he could see his friend clearly. He looked bad, old. His skin was more weathered than he'd ever seen it, his hair—what there was of it—wispy and gray.

He reached over and removed the whiskey bottle from his friend's clutch, and it was a strong clutch. He had to pull a couple of times to get it away from him. It wasn't until he freed the bottle from Cooper's hand that the man stirred, lifted his head, and looked across the table at him, bleary-eyed.

"That you, John?" Cooper rasped.

"It's me, Dale."

Cooper groaned and pushed himself up from the table to an upright position.

"I need a drink," he said.

"Think so?"

"To clear my throat."

Locke hesitated, then pushed his beer mug across to his friend. Cooper hesitated for just a moment, picked it up, and took a healthy swallow. When he was done, he cleared his throat some more, loudly, and pushed the mug back to Locke.

He could smell his friend's foul scent from across the table—whiskey-soaked sweat coming out of his pores.

"Did you ask me to meet you here to see you like this, old friend?" Locke asked.

Cooper cleared his throat one more time, a harsh growl, and then said, "No." He rubbed both hands vigorously over his face. "Christ, John, I need a drink."

"You need some coffee," Locke said, "some food, and a bath, and not in that order."

"A drink first."

"If you take a drink before you do any of those things," Locke said, "I'm going to saddle up and ride out."

"No, no," Cooper said. "Wait. I need you . . . for a job."

"I don't want to hear it, Dale."

"Wh-What?"

"I don't want to hear another word until you're cleaned up and sober," Locke said. "You got any other clothes?"

"Uh, no, no other clothes," the older man said.

"A place to stay?"

"I'm, uh, staying at a roomin' house."

"Been there in a while?"

"Not—not since last night . . . I think."

"Okay," Locke said. "We're going to go over to my hotel and get you cleaned up—and I mean a bath—then we'll go to the general store, and I'll buy you some clothes."

"I've got money," Cooper said, sounding almost indignant.

Locke stood, walked around the table, and took his friend's arm. He helped him to his feet that way, noticing at the same time that Cooper was wearing a gun. It wasn't much of a gun—an old Navy Colt—but it was a gun. He bent down to retrieve Cooper's hat and slapped it down on his head.

"Let's go, Dale," he said, starting for the door.

Abruptly, Cooper pulled his arm away, staggered, and almost fell, but he kept to his feet. "I can walk!"

Locke heard some laughter from the other men, but when he looked over at them, they stopped and looked away.

"Then walk, damn it!" he said. "I didn't come all this way to find out you're a washed-up old drunk."

"Ol' drunk," Cooper muttered. "I'll show you who's an old drunk. Got a job for us, a good one. Good pay."

"I hear from you after ten years of silence because you got a job for us?" Locke asked.

"I need you, John," Cooper said. "I can't do it alone. I need you."

"Fine, Dale," Locke said. "Let's get you that bath and those clothes, and we'll talk about it over a cup of coffee."

"Okay," Cooper said, "okay . . . but I can walk."

"Sure you can," Locke said, and took his arm again.

FIVE

When Dale Cooper was bathed, dressed in new, clean clothes, and reasonably sober, Locke took him to the small café where he'd first met Molly Shillstone.

"Hungry already?" Felix asked.

"My friend could use some coffee," Locke told him, "and I didn't have dessert."

"Pie?"

"Apple," Locke said with a nod. "When's the last time you ate something, Dale?"

"I don't remember."

"Bring two slices," Locke told the waiter.

"Gotcha."

Several tables were occupied, but Locke was able to grab the same table he'd had earlier in the day. Cooper was morose as Locke seated him and then sat across from him.

"You're not making me feel very good about coming all this way to see you, Dale," Locke said. "I dropped what I was doing, even though your telegram said very little, in the name of our friendship. Tell me if you're a hopeless drunk and I'm wasting my time here."

After a moment, Cooper looked across the table at Locke and said, "I'm not hopeless."

"So, you're a drunk."

Cooper said, "My life hasn't been easy since we last saw each other, John."

"And that's why you're a drunk?"

Cooper waited a moment, then said, "I don't remember you being such a harsh judge."

Felix came over with the coffee and pie, saw that something was going on between the two men, and withdrew without saying a word.

"John," Cooper said. "Yes, I am a drunk—or I have been—but I'm trying to quit."

"Didn't look that way to me today, Dale. Looked to me like you spent a few days inside a bottle."

"Don't tell me you've never gotten drunk."

Locke had his own problems with drinking, which had cost him his one and only job as a lawman in Tombstone years ago, but that wasn't the point.

Of course, it had something to do with his being so judgmental when it came to others.

"All right, Dale," Locke said. "The past ten years have been hard on you—so hard that you disappeared from sight. I assume it all stems from that day in Ellsworth?"

"That wasn't my fault," Cooper said.

"You were the marshal," Locke said. "Your fault or not, you took the blame." Much the same thing had happened to Locke in Tombstone, only to a certain extent that was his fault. He wasn't willing to discuss that with Cooper, though. "That was part of the job."

"It wasn't fair," Cooper muttered.

"Eat some pie," Locke said.

"I can't eat."

"Drink some coffee."

"I can't."

"Drink some damn coffee, Dale!"

Cooper lifted the cup to his lips and took a small, grudging sip. Locke ate a bite of apple pie and washed it down with some coffee while continuing to stare across the table at his friend. Cooper's pallor was bad, his eyes were moist, and even the bath had not washed away the smell of whiskey as it continued to leak from his pores.

The man needed help.

"All right, Dale," Locke said. "Why don't you tell me why you asked me to come here?"

SIX

D ale Cooper ate the rest of his pie as he talked, and he had some more coffee.

"The job is delivering a payroll," he explained. He went on to tell Locke what he already knew about Molly Shillstone and her mine. Locke allowed him to go on, though, without telling him that he knew most of the story. As Cooper talked, he seemed to sober up and become animated. He also asked for another slice of pie.

"This is a chance to get back on my feet, John," Cooper said. "They're willing to pay me and whoever I get to help me five hundred dollars apiece. That's more money than I've ever seen, John."

Locke wondered how secure this offer was if Molly Shillstone had approached him— a stranger—about the job.

"This is a done deal?" he asked.

"Completely."

"You don't think that sitting around in the bar the

past few days might have put Mrs. Shillstone off a bit?"

Cooper shrugged. "What does she care what I do in my off time, as long as I get the payroll delivered?"

"What exactly is the job?"

"Pick the payroll up from the train, bring it up the mountain, and deliver it to the manager up there so he can pay the men. It's simple."

"So, the payroll could be hit on the train before it gets here, at the train while we're picking it up, or on the way up the mountain, which is how it was hit last time, right?"

"Right."

"And you think two men can handle this?"

"If the two men are you and me," Cooper said, "yes."

"Coop," Locke said, using the more familiar nickname for the first time, "if I take this job, I've got to know that you can watch my back."

"When have I never watched your back?" Cooper demanded.

"It's been ten years," Locke said. "How do I know how badly your skills may have . . . eroded?"

Cooper glared across the table at Locke, and for the first time, Locke saw the old fire in his friend's eye.

"You want to go outside with me right now and find out how well I can shoot?"

"I don't doubt you can still shoot, Coop," Locke said.

"Then what is it?"

"I'm wondering if you can stay sober."

"Don't worry, John," Cooper said. "For five hundred dollars each, I can stay sober."

Locke hesitated.

"I need you for this, John," Cooper said, shaking his head. "I can't do it with anyone else."

A much truer statement might have been that nobody else would risk it with him.

"All right, Coop," Locke said. "I'm your man."

Cooper sat back and heaved a great sigh of relief. His boozy breath wafted across the table and struck Locke in the face.

"I'll take you over to the mine office and introduce you to Molly Shillstone," he said.

"Let's stop at the general store first," Locke suggested,

"What for?"

"Some peppermint sticks."

"Kids' candy?" Cooper asked. "When did you develop a sweet tooth?"

"It's not for me," Locke said. "I don't want Molly Shillstone smelling that whiskey on your breath."

Cooper put his hand in front of his face and breathed into it, then sniffed his own breath. "You might be right."

"Some lilac water might not be a bad idea, either," Locke said.

"You want me to smell like some fifty-cent whore?"

"Better a fifty-cent whore than a two-bit drunk," Locke said. "I've got to look after my interests, Coop."

Cooper frowned, then said, "Oh, all right!"

They went to the general store, and while they were there, Locke saw that they sold guns.

"We need a gun," he said.

"What for?" Cooper asked.

"For you."

"I got a gun."

"That thing looks like it would explode in your hand, Coop," Locke said. "I'm going to buy you some peppermints and a gun."

"Goddamnit, John," Cooper said, "I tol' you I got money."

"Well, keep it," Locke said. He pointed to a Peacemaker in the display case and told the clerk, "Let me see that one."

"Yes, sir," the clerk said. He took it out and set it on the counter. "A fine weapon, sir, used by—"

"I don't need a sales pitch from a store clerk, friend," Locke said.

"Uh, n-no sir."

Locke picked it, checked the action, and found it satisfactory—to him.

"What do you think?" he asked Cooper, handing the weapon to him. He noticed that his friend's hands still shook some as he accepted the gun. "Fit your hand?"

"It's fine," Coop said, handing it back.

"We'll take it," Locke told the clerk. "And the peppermints."

"Shall I, uh, wrap everything?" the clerk asked.

"No," Locke said. "He'll wear the gun." He took the Navy Colt from his friend's holster and replaced it with the Peacemaker. He was happy to see that all of Cooper's instincts had not deserted him. He immediately removed the gun from his holster and loaded it.

"Here," Locke said, placing the old Navy Colt on the counter. "Get rid of that for me."

SEVEN

As they walked to the Shillstone Mining office, Locke wasn't sure which scent was stronger, peppermint or lilac. Either one was better than the smell of whiskey.

"Are you okay?" Locke asked.

"I'm fine," Cooper said. He stuck a finger in his mouth. "This candy is making my tooth hurt, and the smell of the lilac water is giving me a headache, but I'm fine."

"The price of doing business," Locke said. "I'm just protecting my interests."

They crossed the street and approached the office.

"I should tell you I've already met Molly Shillstone," Locke said.

"When? Where?"

"Earlier today, in that same café," Locke said. "We . . . exchanged pleasantries."

"Did you meet George Crowell?"

"Saw him," Locke said, "but I didn't meet him."

"He's her lapdog," Cooper said. "Supposed to be her manager, but he just goes along with anything she wants."

"Well," Locke said, "she is the owner."

"And a damn fine-lookin' woman."

"She is that."

They reached the door, and Cooper opened it without knocking. He went in first, followed by Locke. Molly Shillstone was behind a desk, and George Crowell was standing in front of it. They both looked at the two men as they entered the room.

"Marshal Cooper," Molly Shillstone said. "And Mr. Locke? What are you doing here?"

"John Locke is the man I've recruited for the job," Cooper said. "And he's accepted."

"Really?" Molly said, raising her eyebrows at Locke. "I had no idea you were connected with the marshal."

"I guess I can say the same about you."

"But I thought we were talking—" George started, but Molly Shillstone cut him off.

"I'm happy that you've agreed to join the marshal," she said. "I'm feeling better about my payroll getting to its destination."

"About that," Cooper said. "Is it still arriving day after tomorrow?"

"Supposedly," Molly said.

"What's that mean?" Locke asked.

"It means that's the plan," Molly said, "but who knows what could happen between now and then?"

"Which train?" Cooper asked.

"There's only one," she said. "The twelve-oh-six."

"We'll be there to meet it," Cooper assured her.

"We'll be where?" Locke asked.

"Kingdom Junction. A day's ride."

Molly came around the desk and stood next to her manager. Locke noticed her wrinkle her nose and knew she'd caught the mixed scents emanating from Dale Cooper.

"Do you have a wagon and a team of horses we'll be able to use?" Cooper asked. "We'll need a good team."

"Out back, Marshal," she said. "George, why don't you take the marshal outside and show him? Mr. Locke and I can use the time to get . . . better acquainted."

George looked as if he were going to object but then simply said, "Oh, all right."

Locke nodded to Cooper, who slowly followed the manager out the front door.

"I don't know what was stronger," Molly said, "the peppermint or the lilac. Your idea?"

"Yes."

"I've heard about his drinking this week," she said. "I was becoming worried."

"Is that why you were going to offer me his job?"

She hesitated, then said, "Would you like a brandy?"

"Why not?"

He watched as she walked to a sideboard and poured two glasses. She was wearing a man's shirt and a skirt and boots with just a hint of skin showing in between. Her hair was still in a bun, but he knew if she let it down, it would fall past her shoulders. Cooper had understated the facts. She was a hell of a lot more than just fine-looking.

She crossed the room and handed him a brandy snifter.

"You're right," she said, going back around her desk. "I was going to offer you his job. I guess it was fate that you end up working for me."

"You're paying me," Locke said, "but I'm doing this for Coop."

"Are you good friends?"

"Yes."

"When was the last time you saw him?"

He hesitated, then said, "A while."

"A long while, I'd wager."

"No bet," Locke said.

She smiled. "Were you shocked when you saw him?"

"Yes," he said, "but there's nobody I'd rather have watching my back than Dale Cooper."

"Even drunk?"

"He won't be drunk."

"Do you guarantee that?"

"Yes."

"Without hesitation," she said. "I admire your loyalty."

"I wouldn't be putting my own life on the line if I didn't think he could handle the job."

"I hope that's the case, Mr. Locke," she said. "If I don't get that money up to my mine, I'm going to be out of business."

"We'll get it up there."

"There are no-goods in this town just waiting for a chance to grab it," she said.

"They'll have to take it away from us."

"They'll try," she said. "That much I'm sure of. You're

going to have to kill a few men to get that money to the mine. Does that bother you at all?"

"If you know who I am, you know that's a silly question," he said. "It'll be their choice to die, not mine."

"Good," she said. "I really do feel better, then. Why don't we celebrate over dinner tonight? My house?"

Locke hesitated, then said, "Coop and I would be happy to have dinner with you."

She tossed her head back and laughed, a sexy, throaty sound.

"Yes, by all means bring the marshal. I'll even invite George. He wants to ride up there with the two of you, you know."

"Is he any good with a gun?"

"They terrify him," she said. "He'd just get all three of you killed. I've told him I need him here."

"That's a good decision."

Locke finished his brandy and moved to her desk, setting the glass down there. "I better go out and have a look at this wagon and team."

"It's a strong buckboard and a good team of horses," she said. "Don't you trust the marshal to inspect them?"

"The buckboard, maybe," Locke said, "but he's a lousy judge of horseflesh."

She laughed again, not quite as heartily as before.

"All right," she said, reaching for her hat. "Let's both go out and have a look."

EIGHT

When they got outside, Molly led Locke around to the back of the building, where there was a corral and a stable. Cooper and Crowell were in the corral, looking over several horses. Both turned when they heard Molly and Locke coming.

"What do you think, John?" Cooper asked. "The gelding and the bay?"

Locke took a moment, then said, "I'd go with both the geldings."

"That one's about ten years old," Cooper said, pointing. "The other one half that."

"That's okay," Locke said. "There's something to be said for experience, don't you think?"

"I definitely agree," Molly said.

"So do I," George Crowell said.

"Fine," Cooper said. "Let's take a look at the buckboard."

"It's in the stable," Crowell said.

"You take a look, Coop," Locke said. "I'll look these horses over a little more closely."

Cooper followed Crowell into the stable.

"The geldings are the two best horses," she said. "They work the best as a team."

Locke ran his hand over one of the geldings and said, "I figured."

"You didn't go into the stable—you're trying to boost his confidence?" she asked.

He turned to face her. "I don't have to boost anything," he said. "Dale Cooper was a great man—a great lawman."

"Once," she said. "I know a drunk when I see one, Mr. Locke. I was married to one."

"Then why would you hire him in the first place?"

"Two reasons," she replied. "First is, he has the experience for this kind of job."

"And the second?"

"I knew he was going to bring someone else in on it," she said. "I was hoping it would be someone from his past, someone with a reputation, someone—well—like you."

"So you have faith in the judgment of a drunk?"

Now she got angry. "There's no one else for the job," she said. "I lost two men when the last payroll was hit—two good men."

"All right," he said. "All right. Reasons aside, Dale and I are here, and we've taken the job. Tell me, how long will it take us to get up the mountain to your mine?"

"With the buckboard?" she asked. "Two days, maybe. I need you to get up there as quickly as possible."

"Why?"

"Rain," she said. "It's been raining harder in the mountains than it has here. That's why our streets are soaked, from the runoff. We built the town far enough away from the mountain to keep from getting flooded. But there's still one major storm coming, and we've got to beat that up the mountain."

"Is it pretty far up?"

"Yes, and it's a rough road to get there," she said. "Not much road at all, in some spots. I've given the marshal two or three different routes."

"You got your mining equipment up there."

"Yes, and lost some men to accidents doing that."

"Wait a minute," Locke said, mentally kicking himself. He was so concerned about Cooper that he was missing some obvious questions. "Why do we even need a buckboard?" he asked. "What's the amount of the payroll?"

Molly Shillstone bit her lip and said, "Eighty thousand."

"Eighty?" Locke was surprised, but still . . . "Even for that much, we shouldn't need a buckboard."

"Marshal Cooper didn't tell you?" she asked.

Locke closed his eyes for a minute. There was a surprise coming, and he hated surprises. "Tell me what, Mrs. Shillstone?"

"My miners are nervous and distrustful," she said. "They want their money in gold."

Shit, he thought.

"And it's Molly."

NINE

"Why didn't you tell me this payroll was in gold?" Locke asked Cooper later in the café. Cooper had wanted to go to the saloon, but Locke vetoed the idea. Now they were seated over cups of coffee instead of glasses of whiskey or mugs of beer.

"I didn't think of it," Cooper said. "I didn't think it would be a problem—do you?"

"Not a problem?" Locke asked. "Do you have any idea what eighty thousand dollars in gold weighs?"

"No."

"Well, neither do I," Locke said, "but it probably is going to take a buckboard to get it up there. That adds a day or more to the trip from Kingdom Junction, and who knows how many days going up the mountain. There's no telling how many times we'll have to turn back to find another way up when we're blocked."

"They'll give us different routes," Cooper said.

"It's a mountain, Coop," Locke said. "Rocks shift and block routes all the time."

"Maybe we can load the gold onto a packhorse," the ex-marshal suggested. "Or two."

"Maybe," Locke said. "We'll just have to wait and see."

"John," Cooper said, "we're getting paid enough to deal with the problems, don't you think?"

"I don't know, Coop," Locke said. "I'll let you know after we've encountered all the problems."

Leaving the café, they parted company. Locke was going to the general store to stock up on ammunition and to purchase other items for the ride, including a good blanket and a slicker. The weather looked as if it was going to continue to rain—another damn problem to overcome.

What they didn't know was that there was another problem keeping an eye on them at the moment.

Robert Bailey huddled in his chosen doorway and watched the two men separate. He left the doorway then and headed for the saloon, where he found two men waiting for him.

When Bailey entered the saloon Hoke Benson and Eli Jordan both looked up from their two-handed game of stud poker. In the middle of the table, at their pot, was a pile of lucifer matchsticks. At each of their elbows was a full mug of beer.

Bailey stopped at the bar to get himself a beer before joining them. "Deal me in."

He took a handful of matches from his vest pocket.

"Well?" Hoke asked.

"Cooper's got John Locke to help him."

Eli gathered up the cards and shuffled them. "That's for sure?" he asked, dealing out three hands of draw poker. They knew that Locke had arrived in town, but they didn't know why.

"Yeah," Bailey said. "I heard 'em talkin' in the café."

"Did they see you?" Eli asked.

"No," Bailey said. "I got across the street before they come out. I bet two."

He tossed in two matchsticks, and both Eli and Hoke called his bet.

"How many cards?" Eli asked.

"Two," Bailey said.

Hoke took three, and so did the dealer.

"So, what do we do?" Bailey asked. "It ain't just a washed-up marshal anymore."

Hoke had a matchstick in his mouth, which he kept shifting from corner to corner. All three men were in their thirties and from behind, according to height and build, might have been related. It was only when you looked at their faces—Hoke handsome, Eli homely, and Robert downright ugly—that you realized they weren't.

"Locke's a little past it, dontcha think?" Hoke asked.

"I heard somethin' about him and Doc Holliday in South Texas," Eli said, "afore Doc died."

"Well," Hoke said, "he ain't got Doc Holliday now, has he?"

"I bet five," Bailey said.

"Still," Eli said. "Hoke?"

"I raise five."

"I call," Eli said.

"Call," Bailey said.

Hoke showed his cards. Three queens.

"Shit," Bailey said, dropping the three tens he'd been dealt onto the table.

"Damn," Eli said, tossing his two pair.

Hoke raked in his matchsticks, took the wet one from his mouth, dropped it onto the floor, and replaced it with one of the new ones.

"We're gonna run outta matchsticks you keep doin' that," Eli said to him.

"We'll have plenty of money to get more when this is all over," Hoke said.

"We got money now," Bailey groused.

"We can't touch it yet," Hoke said. "I told you when we took that first payroll that there would be more."

"I still think it's crazy to stay around and try again," Bailey said.

"You're free to take off, Bob," Eli said.

"Yeah, without my cut of the first job," Bailey said. "You'd like that. You get my cut of the first one and the second one."

"If you're not gonna leave, shut yer mouth and deal," Hoke said.

Bailey shuffled and dealt out cards. "But what're we gonna do about Locke?" he asked without picking up his cards.

Hoke let his cards lie, too. "Look," he said, "the second payroll's gonna be two or three times the size of the first one, maybe more. There's enough money to go around."

"Meanin' what?" Eli asked.

"Meanin' we can get a couple of more men if you fellas are afraid of a washed-up lawman and an over-the-hill gunman."

"Over the hill or not," Eli said, "he's still the Widowmaker."

Bailey frowned. "I thought the gun was called the Widowmaker."

"Either way," Eli said, "don't make much difference. It's still him." He looked at Hoke. "I say we get at least two more men."

Hoke looked at Bailey. "What about you?"

"Sounds like a good idea to me."

Hoke picked up his cards and looked at them, then folded them into a pile in his hands. Bailey looked at his, followed by Eli.

"I open for two," Eli said.

"I raise five," Hoke said.

"Yer bluffin'," Bailey said. "I call the seven."

"I call, too," Eli said.

"How many cards, Eli?" Bailey asked.

"Just one," Eli said. "Got me a good hand."

Bailey dealt Eli his cards, then looked at Hoke.

"I'll play these."

"A pat hand?" Bailey asked.

"That's what I've got," Hoke said. He had no expression on his face for the other two men to read.

"Damn," Bailey said. "I'll take three."

"I check to the raiser," Eli said.

"Thought you had a good hand?" Hoke asked.

"Not as good as a pat hand."

"He's bluffin'," Bailey said.

"I bet twenty," Hoke said, pushing twenty lucifers into the pot.

Bailey bit his lip, looked at his cards, and said, "I'll call."

"Me, too," Eli said. "Let's see 'em."

Hoke put down four deuces, and an ace.

"Four of a kind?" Bailey said. "Shee-it." He tossed his cards onto the table, facedown.

"Why didn't you take one card?" Eli asked, dropping his two pair facedown.

"How would that improve my hand?" Hoke asked, raking in his sticks. "I didn't need another card."

"Okay," he said. "We'll bring in two more men, but they don't get any cut from the first job."

"That's fair," Eli said.

"Maybe we shouldn't even tell them anything about the first job," Bailey said.

"Everybody knows the first payroll was hit," Hoke said.

"They don't know it was us, though," Eli said.

"That's true," Hoke said, shuffling the cards, "but anybody we bring in is gonna figure us for the first one."

"So, what do we do?" Bailey asked.

"We let 'em figure what they want," Hoke said, "and we don't tell 'em nothin'." He dealt out the cards. "We just keep our mouths shut about the first job. Agreed?"

"Agreed," Eli said.

"Bob?"

Bailey looked up from his cards and said, "Huh? Oh, yeah, I agree." Nervously, he picked up five matchsticks and tossed them into the pot. "I bet five."

Eli looked at Hoke, and both men said, "I fold."

TEN

Locke made sure that Cooper was sober and clean when they walked to Molly Shillstone's house for dinner. He had bought them each a slicker so they'd be dry for dinner. It was still drizzling when they made their walk, and Molly took their slickers when she answered the door.

They had passed some homes along the way, and Molly's was easily the largest in town—two stories and built with good, new lumber rather than reused wood, like many of the others. In other words, she had an honest-to-God house, not a shack.

"Somethin' smells good," Cooper said as they entered.

"I'm a good cook as well as a good businesswoman," Molly told them. "Please, come into the living room."

They followed her into a sparsely furnished room with bare floors. George Crowell was seated on a sofa, holding a glass of brandy.

"I had the furniture brought in from St. Louis," she said. "There's not much of it, but I'm not finished."

"You must plan on being here awhile," Locke observed.

"I don't anticipate my mine playing out for quite some time," she said.

She had poured two brandies and carried them to the two men. Before Locke could stop him, Cooper had accepted. He didn't think Molly knew what she was doing.

"I have to check on dinner," she said. "I'm sure George will keep you entertained."

As she left the room, Locke and Cooper looked at George Crowell. He was duded up in a suit and tie, while Locke and Cooper simply had their best trail clothes on.

"Don't have a suit with me," Cooper said lamely.

"That's all right," Crowell said.

"She seems to be a remarkable woman," Locke commented.

"She's more than that," Crowell said. "She's amazing."

"Have you worked for her long?"

"I worked for her father. I've been with her for years now," he said. "We came here to Turnback Creek together."

"Is there one?" Locke asked.

"One what?" Crowell asked.

"Creek."

"Yes," the man said. "You'll cross it on your way to the mine."

Locke knew the question had been inane, but this was not where he was at his best. He'd accepted the invitation because he wanted to get to know Molly Shillstone and her manager a little better if he was going to risk his life taking their payroll up the mountain for five hundred dollars.

Cooper walked over to an overstuffed chair and sat down. For Locke's money, the man was paying entirely too much attention to his drink. Also, sitting in that chair put him closer to the decanter the brandy had come out of.

Locke remained standing. "Mr. Crowell," he said, "why don't you tell us what you know about the first payroll that got hit?"

"There's not much to tell," the man replied. "It didn't arrive at the mine so they sent some men out to look for it. They found the two men who were delivering it dead along the way, and the payroll was gone."

"How were they killed?"

"Shot."

"Where?" Locke asked.

"Um, out in the open."

"I mean, in the back? Front?"

"Oh, I see," Crowell said. "I'm not sure, but I don't remember anything about them being shot in the back."

"I'll check with the sheriff tomorrow," Locke said, "or the undertaker. You do have an undertaker, don't you?"

"Oh, uh, yes, of course we do," Crowell said. "I'm sure he'll be able to help you with that."

At that point, Molly came out of the kitchen and announced, "If you'll all come to the dining room, dinner is served."

Locke made sure he got between Cooper and the brandy decanter on the way.

ELEVEN

Molly had made a perfect pot roast, surrounded by all kinds of vegetables. She also announced that there was a pie in the oven for dessert.

During the dinner conversation, Locke learned that Molly's father, Arthur Shillstone, had started the family in the mining business and that George Crowell had worked for him for many years. When her father died, Molly took over the business.

"That was five years ago," she said. "This mine has been my most successful to date. That's why I can't afford to have my people walk out on me. I've got everything invested in this mine."

She seemed so sincere Locke wondered why she had been so willing to depend on Cooper—even if all she was depending on him to do was bring in someone like Locke.

He suddenly realized that not only Molly Shillstone's but, apparently, her father's life's work depended almost solely on him. He was going to have to make sure that Cooper stayed sober—and he also had to find out just how much ex-Marshal Dale Cooper had left.

After dinner, Molly served up slices of huckleberry pie and cups of coffee. Following that, the men repaired to the front porch, where George Crowell produced cigars, which Locke and Cooper accepted.

"I wanted to go with you, you know," Crowell finally said.

"That's what Molly said," Locke answered.

"You can come," Cooper said.

"She doesn't want me to."

"He'd be in too much danger, Dale," Locke said. "He doesn't handle a gun well."

"I don't handle a handgun at all," Crowell said, "but I can use a rifle pretty—"

"That's okay, George," Locke said. "Coop and I can handle it."

"We don't really have any idea how many men hit the first payroll," Crowell said.

"Did the sheriff ride out there to have a look?" Locke asked.

"He did."

"Well, then, we need to talk to him," Locke said, looking at Cooper. "See what he was able to figure out."

"That's right," Cooper said. "We'll talk to him tomorrow."

Locke noticed that the hand Cooper was holding the cigar with was trembling.

"Maybe we should be getting along," he said. "We're going to have an early day tomorrow, getting ready for Friday." That was the day the payroll was supposed to be arriving at the railhead.

"You can't leave yet," Molly said, coming out the door behind them. "I haven't had my cigar yet."

She walked over to Crowell, who took out another cigar, snipped the end for her, and held a match to it while she got it going to her satisfaction.

"How long have you smoked cigars?" Locke asked. He assumed she was trying to shock them.

"I used to light them for my father all the time," she said. "And I mean that I would snip the ends, put it in my mouth, and get it going for him. I always liked the taste." She drew on the cigar and exhaled the smoke in a blue cloud. "I have one every so often now."

"I see."

She smiled. "You thought I was doing it for shock value?"

"Well . . ."

"I don't do anything for shock value, Mr. Locke—may I call you John?"

"Why not?"

"With me, John," she said, "what you see is what I am. I don't know any other way to act."

"Then we have that in common, Molly," Locke said. "I'm very much the same way."

*   *   *

Locke finally grabbed Cooper and headed back to the hotel.

"Why don't we stop in the saloon—" Cooper started.

"I don't think that's a good idea, Coop."

"Just one drink before turning in, John," Cooper said. "I keep earlier hours these days, anyway."

"Dale," Locke said, "a lot of people's lives and livelihoods are riding on this—not to mention ours. I don't want to take any unnecessary chances, do you?"

"I suppose not."

"That glass of brandy you had tonight?"

"Yes."

"Let's consider that your last drink for a while."

"What?" Cooper asked. "That wasn't even a decent drink."

"Look," Locke said, grabbing his friend's arm and stopping both their progress. "I saw your hand shaking tonight just holding that cigar. How's it going to be when you have to hold a gun?"

"I'll be fine."

"Well, I want to find out for sure," Locke said. "You and I are going to do some target shooting in the morning, so you better get yourself a good night's sleep."

"John—"

"If you can't hit what you aim at tomorrow, Dale," Locke said, "I'm out. You got that?"

"We're getting five hundred doll—"

"I'm not doing this for the money, Coop," Locke said. "I'm doing it out of friendship—but I'm not getting killed for friendship, understand?"

"All right," Cooper said. "I understand. I'll go back to my room and get a good night's sleep. Tomorrow you'll see I'm as good with a gun as I ever was. Better than you, if you remember."

"I remember," Locke said, and they continued on to the hotel.

TWELVE

Once they were in their hotel rooms, Locke had a look out his window. He hadn't seen anyone, but he had the feeling all day that someone was watching them. Word had probably gotten out that they were going to escort the payroll up to the mine, just the two of them. If they had more time, Locke would have considered bringing someone else in, somebody about whose ability with a gun he had no doubt. Tomorrow would tell just how much he was going to be able to depend on Dale Cooper.

Locke couldn't see anyone from his window, but all the doorways across from the hotel were dark. He was considering whether or not to go to the nearest saloon. His one-beer-a-day limit had been reached already, and some brandy had already been added to that, but he wasn't ready to turn in. Maybe he'd even pick up some useful information.

He successfully talked himself into leaving the hotel and walking over to the Three Aces Saloon.

When he walked into the Three Aces, the place was in full swing. Music came from a corner piano, poker and faro were being played all around him, and in another part of the room, a roulette wheel was spinning. Even above the din, he could hear the ball bouncing around.

He walked to the bar, elbowed his way in, and ordered a beer. The bartender from that afternoon, Al, was not working. A man standing next to him turned to look at him, apparently didn't like what he saw, and looked away, giving Locke as much room at the bar as he could.

Locke turned to face the room, holding his beer mug in his hand. Three girls were working the room, all tired-looking but attractive. He wasn't interested in women at the moment, though. He was checking to see if anyone was interested in him.

Throughout his life, John Locke was a man who either drew stares or caused men to avert their eyes. At the moment, no one seemed to be looking at him, but on the way to the saloon from his hotel, he'd still had the sensation of being watched—not necessarily followed but definitely watched.

As he worked on his beer, the batwing doors swung inward, and Sheriff Hammet entered. He stopped just inside the door, looked around, spotted Locke, and came walking over. "Mr. Locke," he said.

"Sheriff."

The sheriff reached past Locke and accepted a cold

beer from the bartender. "I've been hearing interesting things about you and the marshal," Hammet said.

"Have you?" Locke asked. "Like what?"

"Like you're working for Molly Shillstone," Hammet said. "Gonna deliver her payroll day after tomorrow."

"We're going to try."

"You and Marshal Cooper, right?" the lawman asked. "Just the, uh, two of you?"

"That's right."

"You're a brave man."

"Why's that?"

"Takin' all that money up the mountain with only a drunk to watch your back?"

"I'd rather have Dale Cooper watching my back than any man alive," Locke said coldly.

Hammet backed off. "Hey, no offense meant," he said.

"Offense taken."

"Let me buy you another beer to make up for it."

"I'm still working on this one."

"I was just goin' by what I saw," the lawman said. "Your Marshal Cooper has been here for some time. I didn't know who he was, but he really didn't lift his head up off the table very often."

"I know a way you can make it up."

"How?"

"Tell me about the first payroll being hit."

"Not much to tell," the sheriff said with a shrug. "Molly sent two of her own up there, and they were ambushed."

"Back shot?"

"One of 'em, yeah," Hammet said.

"Any sign up there?"

"I ain't much for reading sign on rocks," the lawman said, "but near as I can figure, there was two of 'em."

"Nobody came forward with any information?" Locke asked. "Nobody was flashing money, maybe gambling beyond their means?"

"I'm just a humble mining-town lawman, Mr. Locke," Hammet said. "I ain't no detective. All I can say is, somebody hit that payroll and got away with it. Nothin' I can do about it."

"And I guess you'll say the same thing if this second one is hit, too," Locke commented.

"I'm afraid so."

"So, Cooper and I are on our own."

"And getting paid for the privilege, as I understand it—probably more than I make in a year," Hammet said. "I ain't about to go up that mountain with a bunch of money and risk my life for my salary."

"I can't blame you for that," Locke said.

"Nice of you to say."

Sheriff Hammet finished his beer and set the empty mug back on the bar top.

"I wish you both luck," he said, "and I hope I won't be cartin' both your bodies down the mountain."

Locke didn't comment, but he had the same hope.

THIRTEEN

After Locke and Cooper left Molly Shillstone's house, she and George Crowell sat together on the porch. Molly knew George was waiting for her to invite him to stay overnight. He always waited for that invitation, and it never came—and never would. She often wondered why he didn't know that. He was older than she and not the least bit attractive. In addition, he was weak. He had attached himself to her father for years, and now he was doing the same thing to her. If and when she found herself a real man, someone who would marry her and be at least as strong as she was, George Crowell would be out of a job. For now, he had his uses—but warming her bed was not one of them.

"Are you sure you want to do this, Molly?"

"Hmm? Do what, George?"

"Entrust all this gold to these two men," he said. "What do we know about them?"

"Well, quite a bit, actually," she said, "They do both have rather big reputations."

"Yes, as gunmen."

"Marshal Cooper's is more as a lawman than a gunman," Molly pointed out. "Mr. Locke, as I understand it, has more of a reputation as a gunman. The Widowmaker, they call him. Or is that what they call his gun?"

"Nevertheless," he said, "Cooper is more of a drunk right now than anything else."

"He had one glass of brandy tonight, that I saw," Molly said. "Not exactly what you'd expect from a drunk, George."

"Molly, his hands were shaking out here on the porch."

"I trust Mr. Locke's judgment," she said. "If he deems the marshal fit to go up the mountain with, that's good enough for me. Why would he risk his life with a drunk?"

Crowell turned in his chair to face her. "Molly, why would you put so much faith in a stranger?"

"I have a good feeling about him."

"You're attracted to him," Crowell accused.

She didn't answer.

"That's what it is, isn't it?"

"George," she said, "I think it's time we said good night."

Crowell lived in a small shack near the mining office. Molly had never been inside and did not intend ever to be.

"Molly—"

"Good night, George." She said it without looking at him. Slowly, he got up from his chair, stepped off the porch, and left.

Molly closed her eyes for a moment, imagining that John Locke had been watching, waiting for George to leave so he could come back, come to her bed. Locke was the kind of man she'd been waiting for all her life, despite the fact that he was much older than she was. She wondered what kind of woman he'd been waiting for.

Hoke Benson watched from across the room while John Locke and the sheriff had a conversation. There were enough men sitting between him and the bar that he felt certain Locke would not be able to see him. He just wanted to take some time to observe the man. Hoke was still trying to decide if they should hit the payroll at the train, between Turnback Creek and the train, or on the mountain. He was also waiting to hear from the other men he'd "invited" to participate in the robbery to get back to him. Word had gotten out that it was John Locke who was taking the money up the mountain. There weren't a lot of men who wanted to go up against the Widowmaker, but Hoke felt sure that in the end, the money would overcome their fear. Besides, wherever they did it, they were going to ambush Locke and Cooper, so the two old legends would never know what hit them.

The lawman left, and Locke stayed for a few moments before also leaving. Eli and Bailey were playing faro, but Hoke left them alone. He didn't feel there was any need to follow Locke back to his hotel. They had all day tomorrow to keep an eye on the man.

*　*　*

Locke watched the lawman leave, then finished his own beer and set the empty mug on the bar.

" 'Nother one?" the bartender asked.

Locke was tempted. In two days' time, he was going to put his life on the line for five hundred dollars. That was a lot of money to Dale Cooper—a lot more than it was to Locke. In all Cooper's years as a lawman, he had probably never made that much money in one year. He certainly had not seen that much at one time during the past ten years. But it wasn't enough to John Locke to risk his life for.

Now, his friendship with Dale Cooper, that was something worth risking his life for, but that didn't mean he wouldn't be nervous about it. A lot would depend on how Cooper performed with his gun tomorrow—a new gun in a shaky hand, at that.

The bartender was still waiting for a reply.

"No," Locke finally said. "No more, thanks."

After riding Cooper all day about his drinking, the last thing Locke could do was get drunk himself. And it would be an easy thing to do—a far too easy thing to do—to have another beer, and then another, and then just keep going and going . . .

Locke stiffened, straightened up from the bar, and forced himself to walk out the front door and go back to his hotel room for the night. Even in his room, and in his bed, that next beer was still calling to him.

FOURTEEN

The next morning, Locke left his hotel and walked down the street to the rooming house where Dale Cooper was staying. He hoped the ex-marshal had been able to stay in his room last night and had not sneaked out to any of the saloons. If he had, then Locke was prepared to saddle up and head out of town. Leaving Molly Shillstone in the lurch was no problem for him. She'd get somebody else to deliver her gold, or get killed trying to do it. Locke's only reason for being involved was to try to help Cooper regain some of his self-esteem and possibly some of his lost stature.

He went up the walk to the two-story rooming house, mounted the porch, and knocked on the door. Out of all the homes he'd seen in town, this was the only one built nearly as well as Molly Shillstone's house.

An elderly woman answered the door, and he asked politely for Dale Cooper.

"The marshal is having his breakfast," the woman said.

"Oh," Locke said. "I was going to buy him breakfast."

"Well, I'm Mrs. Helms, and this is my house," she said. "You're welcome to come in and eat with him. There's plenty of food."

"That's very kind of you, ma'am," Locke said, removing his hat. "Thank you."

He entered, and she closed the door.

"I don't have any other boarders at the moment," she said. "Come this way."

He followed her into the dining room, where Cooper was digging into a pile of flapjacks. Also on the table were plates of scrambled eggs, bacon, and fresh biscuits. The aroma of coffee was heady.

"Marshal, you have a guest."

Cooper looked up from the table and smiled when he saw Locke standing there.

"Pull up a chair, John," he invited. "Ingrid makes the best breakfast in town."

"That coffee smells mighty good, ma'am."

"I'll get you a cup," she said. "You just set and dig in."

"Thank you."

Locke sat across the table from Cooper and was amazed at how well rested the man looked. He was eating heartily and looked like a completely different man from the day before.

"Coop, I've got to say you look . . . changed."

Cooper waved his fork. "I've given up the bottle, John. Look at my hands." He held them out, and they were as steady as a rock.

"Just like that?"

"It's time to go to work," Cooper said. "I don't drink when I'm working."

Ingrid Helms came back into the room and poured Locke a cup of coffee. Then she walked over to Cooper and refilled his cup, leaning on his shoulder with one hand. She appeared to Locke to be older than the marshal, but he wondered if the two had formed some sort of a relationship.

He helped himself to bacon and eggs and biscuits, intending to follow that with some of the flapjacks.

"You're gonna be wantin' to see me shoot today, right?" Cooper asked.

"That's right."

"That's why I gave up the bottle. My hands have got to be steady to show you I'm as good as I ever was."

Locke wondered if Cooper had had a drink that morning. Very often, the hair of the dog that bit him will brace a man, but Cooper's eyes seemed very clear.

"Will you gentlemen be wanting any more food?" Mrs. Helms asked at one point.

"Ma'am," Locke said, "I do believe you've got enough food here to feed an army, and might I say I haven't had a better meal since . . . well, since I can't remember when."

"You should move in here," Cooper said. "You could eat like this every day."

"You'd be most welcome, sir," Mrs. Helms said. "Are you staying at the hotel?"

"Yes, ma'am."

"Be cheaper here, and you'd eat better."

"I can see that, ma'am," he said. "Fact is, we'll be leavin' tomorrow to pick up Mrs. Shillstone's payroll, and then we'll be taking it up the mountain to the mine."

"Might there be anything you'd be leaving behind?" she asked. "It'd be safer here than at that hotel."

"She's got a point there, John," Cooper said, with a jabbing motion of his fork.

"All right, then," Locke said. "I'll move my stuff here from the hotel later today."

"That'll be fine," she said. "I'll give you the room right next to the marshal's."

Locke felt the least he could do for this meal was give the woman another boarder.

"Now, you gents just eat up, and I'll go upstairs and get your friend's room ready."

"His name is Locke, Ingrid," Cooper said. "John Locke, and he's the best friend a man ever had."

"Well, I'm glad you have a friend like Mr. Locke, then, Marshal," she said. "It appears to me you're gonna need him."

FIFTEEN

After breakfast, Ingrid Helms showed Locke where his room was, and he promised not to come back too late to move in. He and Cooper then left the rooming house together.

"I don't remember the last time I was so stuffed," Locke said.

"Good thing we're leaving tomorrow," Cooper said. "A man could get fat staying there."

"Coop, I've got to say, I'm still stunned by the change in you," Locke said.

"I tol' you," the older man answered, "I don't drink while I'm workin'. Far as I'm concerned, this is the first day of the job."

"Well, I'm glad to hear it," Locke said. "I feel much better about this job now."

"Wait until you see me shoot," Cooper said. "You'll be feelin' even better."

They found an area out behind the hotel where they'd be able to do some target shooting without anyone being hit by a stray bullet. Others obviously had used the area for the same purpose, as there were broken bottles of varying sizes around, as well as previously perforated cans.

"I'll set some up," Locke said. He collected the largest chunks of bottles he could find and set them up on some rocks—five in all. He returned to Cooper's side. "Let's see how this new gun of yours shoots."

"You want me to draw and fire?" Cooper asked when Locke came and stood alongside him.

"Just hit them, and I'll be happy," Locke said.

Cooper drew his gun from his holster and fired three shots. Two bottles shattered, and one bullet ricocheted off a rock.

"Damn!" Cooper said.

"That's okay," Locke said. "It might be the gun, not you."

"The gun is fine," Cooper said. "It shoots true."

He fired the other three shots in the cylinder, and one of the other cans flew off.

"Goddamnit!"

"It's okay, Coop—"

"Okay ain't good enough!" Cooper snapped. "Okay ain't gonna keep you alive if I can't hit what I'm shootin' at. You wouldn'ta missed a damn one of them!"

Locke walked over to the bottles and cans and set up two bottles. "There's two more bottles," Locke said, returning to his friend's side. "Take the both of them."

Cooper licked his lips and reloaded the weapon. He

extended his arm and fired deliberately this time. Both bottles shattered.

"There you go," Locke said.

Cooper ejected the spent shells from his Colt and replaced them with live ones.

"A man ain't gonna stay still like a bottle," Cooper said. "I ain't gonna have time to aim."

He holstered his gun and walked around collecting cans. He went and set them up where the bottles had been, then returned to stand next to Locke. "Six cans," he said. "You take the three on the right, I'll take the three on the left."

"Coop—"

"Just do it, will ya?" Cooper snapped.

Locke sighed. "All right."

"On three," Cooper said. "One . . . two . . . three . . ."

Both men drew their weapons. One of Cooper's cans flew off the rock first, but all three of Locke's quickly followed. Once again, Cooper had left one can behind.

"You beat me," Locke said, ejecting the spent shells.

"Fast don't mean better," Cooper said, doing the same. "I want to go again."

"Coop," Locke said, holstering his gun, "I'm satisfied that you can shoot well—"

"If I was you," Cooper said, interrupting him, "I wouldn't want to go up that mountain with me coverin' your back. Not the way I'm shootin'."

"Maybe with some more practice—"

"We ain't got time to practice," Cooper said, cutting him off. "We gotta go and pick up that payroll tomorrow."

"I know, but—"

"And there's a good chance somebody'll try to take it from us before we even get to the mountain," Cooper went on. "You know that. The first payroll was such easy pickin's, I'll bet there's two or three gangs just waterin' at the mouth to come at us."

"If they do," Locke said, "we'll handle them."

"Yeah, right."

Cooper turned to face the can he'd left standing. He drew quickly and fired from the hip. The can went flying.

"That's better," he said. "More like it."

"Keep shooting," Locke said. "We've got time today. By the end of the day, you'll be hitting five out of five."

"Six out of six," Cooper said, replacing the single spent shell. "I ain't gonna be happy with nothin' less."

"I know you won't, Coop," Locke said.

"Just keep shootin' with me, John."

"I wouldn't want to be shooting with anyone else, Coop," John Locke told him.

SIXTEEN

Later in the day, Cooper was still missing a shot here and there and was not happy with his performance. Locke also noticed that the man was constantly licking his lips and wiping them with the back of his hand, a sure sign that he was craving a drink. It seemed that nothing he said to the ex-marshal helped much at all.

"Coop," Locke said at one point, "you're shooting better than most men could ever hope to."

"It's not enough, John," Cooper said. "Not nearly good enough. If I expect you to watch my back, you've got to be able to expect me to watch yours."

Locke put his hand on his old friend's shoulder and said, "Believe me, there's nobody I'd rather have watching my back."

"Sure there is," Cooper said. "The man I was fifteen years ago."

"Why that far back?" Locke asked. "Why not ten years ago?"

"Not ten years ago," Cooper said. "You remember why . . ."

Ellsworth, Kansas
1877

Marshal Dale Cooper and John Locke walked to the end of the street shoulder to shoulder. Waiting for them there were five cowboys from the Bar Z spread, who had driven their cattle in only the day before. These five had gotten particularly drunk the night before in the Alhambra Saloon, shot the place up, and injured one man, an innocent bystander. Cooper had arrived on the scene after the men had fled. He talked with the foreman, Bud Selkirk, and told him that the five men should give themselves up the next day at noon. Selkirk told Cooper that the men would be waiting at the north end of Main Street but that it would be up to them whether or not they came peaceably.

"They's Texas cowboys, Marshal," he said. "No tellin' what they'll do."

"Won't they do what you tell 'em to?" Cooper asked.

"On a trail drive, yeah," Selkirk said. "But in a situation like this, when one, two, or all of 'em might go to jail? No. I'd suggest you take a deputy or two with you."

Well, Cooper didn't have a deputy or two who were willing to face five Texas cowpokes with him. What he did have was his friend John Locke, and that was enough for him.

But there was something Locke didn't know. Cooper himself had been drinking the night before, and for some time. His insides were jittery, and his hands were shaking. He told Locke he wanted to take the men in with no gunplay but that according to what the foreman had told him, it was going to be up to them.

John Locke would stand by his friend and back his play, no matter what . . .

When they reached the north end of Main Street, Locke saw the five cowboys standing abreast. As he got closer, he could see by the looks on their faces that some of them were nervous. What bothered him was that he could also feel Cooper's nerves. As long as he'd known Marshal Dale Cooper, he'd had nerves of steel. Why was today different?

"You men need to give yourselves up without any fuss," Cooper announced to the five cowboys.

"We didn't mean to hurt nobody, Marshal," one of them called out.

"I know that," Cooper said. "It was just end-of-the-trail hijinks that got outta hand. But somebody did get hurt, and I got to take you in."

To Locke, all five cowboys now looked scared. Three of them were barely twenty, and they seemed to be looking to the two older men for guidance.

"Are we gonna go to jail?" one of the younger ones asked. "I can't go to jail, Marshal."

"That's not for me to decide, boy," Cooper said. "Just drop your guns to the ground, and we'll walk over to the jail."

The youngster who was afraid of going to jail said to his compadre, "Ned, I can't go to jail."

"Take it easy, Harve—"

But young Harve panicked, and he went for his gun. The situation still could have been handled, in Locke's view, but Cooper reacted. He cleanly outdrew the boy and shot him dead when he probably didn't have to. In hindsight, Locke saw the boy freeze as Cooper's gun cleared leather so quickly. It could have ended there, but Cooper pulled the trigger, and then everybody was shooting, including Locke . . .

"I killed some of those cowboys, too, Coop," Locke reminded his friend now.

"Yeah, you did," Cooper said. "But I fired the first shot. The town council didn't want a lawman who was trigger-happy, who had started drinkin'—"

"Nobody knew that."

"Somebody did," Cooper said.

"I feel bad that I didn't," Locke said. "We're friends. I should have known something was wrong."

"Not your fault, John," Cooper said. "After they took my badge away, I just crawled into a bottle, and I only come out a few months ago. I heard about this job and thought, this is my chance. I can make some money and get back some of my self-respect, maybe get some of my reputation back."

"Then that's what we'll do, Dale," Locke said. "We'll do all of it."

"Not with me shootin' this way."

"Look," Locke said, "let's take a break, get some coffee, and talk about what we're going to do tomorrow. After that, if you want to come back out here and shoot some more, I'm with you."

Cooper looked at Locke. "You been holdin' back," he accused.

"Coop—"

"Ain'tcha?"

"I'm no sharpshooter, Coop," Locke said, shaking his head, "but I can hit what I shoot at."

"Wait."

Cooper set up four cans and two bottles, then returned to where Locke was standing.

"Hit all six, and then we'll go and have coffee."

Locke took a deep breath, then drew his gun—not for speed but just to get it out—and fired six measured shots. All six cans and bottles went flying or shattered.

"I'll buy," Cooper said.

SEVENTEEN

Cooper cooled off some over coffee at the café. "Let me tell you something," Locke told him. "The Dale Cooper I saw yesterday couldn't have gotten his gun out of his holster without shooting his foot off. Give yourself another couple of days off the whiskey, and you'll probably be fine."

"You might be right," Cooper said, and Locke thought at that point the man might let up on himself some.

"I have an idea about moving the gold," he said, changing the subject.

"Let's hear it."

"Once we collect the gold from the train in Kingdom Junction, we're going to have to camp one night between here and there."

"So?"

"So, I think we should bypass this town the next day and head straight up the mountain."

"I'm sure Molly's gonna want to see her gold."

"Then she can meet us somewhere and take a look at it," Locke said. "Crowell said we're going to have to cross the creek to get to the mountain, right?"

"That's right."

"Do you know where the actual creek is?"

"Outside of town a few miles," Cooper replied, "between here and the mountain."

"Fine," Locke said. "Then she can meet us there, inspect her gold shipment, and we can get moving. That way, nobody gets a chance to try for us right here in town."

Cooper gave it some thought, then said, "All right, I like it. What about the law?"

"What about him?"

"Should we let him in on our plans?"

"I know you were a lawman for a long time, Coop," Locke said, "but I don't trust this one."

"Why not?"

"He feels . . . wrong."

"Well," Cooper said, "I don't like goin' around the law, but I'll trust your judgment. So, we just tell Molly?"

"Right," Locke said.

"What about Crowell?"

"No. Let's keep control of who knows what we're doing."

"What if she tells him?"

"We'll have to stress the importance of not telling anyone," Locke said. "I think she'll understand. She's a smart woman."

"She's a smart woman," Cooper said, "with eyes for you."

"What are you talking about?"

"Hey," the ex-marshal said. "Even an old drunk can see that."

"I'm not here to find a woman, Coop."

"You could do worse."

"I've been alone a long time," Locke said, "and I intend to stay that way. I like it."

Cooper regarded his friend across the table. "You never found a woman you wanted to settle down with? In all these years?"

"I'm as settled as I'm ever going to be in Las Vegas," Locke said. "I got a nice little place there, and I'm not looking to share it with anyone else. I'm comfortable."

"That's sad."

"Why sad?" Locke asked. "Have you got a woman?"

"No."

"Ever had a woman?"

"No, but I was a lawman for a lot of years, like you said," Cooper answered. "That's no life for a woman."

"Well, my life is certainly no life for a woman, either," Locke said. "So, I guess we're just destined to stay old bachelors." Cooper lifted his coffee cup, and Locke followed. They clinked them, and Locke said, "Here's to old bachelors."

They drained their coffee cups, set them down, and Cooper said, "Now, let's go shoot some more."

EIGHTEEN

When they left the café, they decided to go right to Molly's office to discuss their plan. She was there alone, without Crowell, which allowed them to talk freely after she greeted them, and they exchanged pleasantries about the dinner the night before.

"It's a good thing we don't eat like that every day," Cooper said, touching his stomach.

"Don't either of you have a . . . wife to cook for you?" she asked, looking at Locke.

"Uh, no," he said, thinking about what Cooper had said. "I've never been married."

"I never have, either," Cooper said, but Molly wasn't listening to him. She was obviously more interested in what Locke had to say.

"No woman waiting for you where you live?" she asked Locke.

"Um, no," he said, feeling uncomfortable. "We want to

discuss something with you, Molly . . . about the gold."

"I see." She seemed amused at his discomfort. She sat back in her chair. "All right, gentlemen, what's on your minds? I know you came here to tell me something."

Locke allowed Cooper to explain their plan. He was, after all, the lead man on this job.

She listened intently, nodding but not saying a word until Cooper was finished.

"I like it," she said. "In fact, I wholeheartedly agree with it. I'll meet you Sunday afternoon at Turnback Creek. Do you think you can be there by three in the afternoon?"

Locke looked at Cooper, because he was the one who knew how far away Kingdom Junction was.

"I think it would be hard to pinpoint our arrival that much," Cooper said, "but we should be able to make it by afternoon."

"Very well, then."

"There's one more thing," Locke said.

"What's that?"

"We don't think anyone else should know about this," he said. "Just the three of us.

"Not the sheriff?"

"Especially not the sheriff," Locke said. He explained how he got a bad feeling from the man.

"I think you're right," she said. "He didn't do much about finding the men who grabbed my first payroll. We probably can't count on him for any kind of help."

"And let's not give him any unnecessary information," Locke said. "That way, if something happens, we won't have to view him with any suspicion. If only the three of us know, then nothing can go wrong."

"All right," she said. "We leave the sheriff out of the loop. But I have to tell George."

"Why?" Locke asked. "Why do you have to?"

She stared at him for a minute, then said, "I don't know. I usually discuss everything with him."

"Well, maybe not this," Locke said.

She sat forward. "Are you telling me you suspect George—"

"I don't suspect him of anything," Locke said. "We're just trying to keep down the number of people who know what we're doing. What if he let something slip by accident? Perhaps in the saloon?"

"You'll hardly ever find George in a saloon," she said, "but I can see what you mean."

"We're responsible for this gold, Molly," Cooper said. "We feel we have the right to make some . . . requests."

"Or demands," she said. She bit her lip for a moment. "All right, I'll keep George in the dark."

"Is there any problem with you riding from here to the creek alone?" Locke asked.

She smiled and said, "No. I'm an accomplished rider, John, and I'm not the nervous type. I'll be able to ride out there, and if I get there before you do, I can make camp and wait. I don't mind spending some time alone."

"That's good," Cooper said.

"Well," Locke said, moving toward the door, "we still have some preparations to make."

"You have a line of credit at the general store," she

said. "Just tell Herman Hollaway that you work for me."

"Thanks," Cooper said. "We'll do that."

"Let me walk you out." She went out the front door with them, then tugged on Locke's sleeve before he could leave. "Could I talk to you a moment?"

Locke looked to Cooper for help, but the ex-marshal simply said, "I'll meet you at the store."

Cooper stepped down and walked away as Locke turned to face Molly Shillstone.

"I was wondering if you'd like to have dinner at my house again tonight," she said. "This time without George and the marshal?"

"I don't think that's a good idea, Molly."

"Why not?"

"We have to get an early start in the morning," he said. "The kind of meal we had last night tends to make a man . . . lazy. In my business, lazy means dead."

"Well, maybe just drinks, then?"

"Uh, I don't think—"

"Mr. Locke," she asked, "do I make you nervous?"

Locke stared at her for a moment, her smooth skin and pretty eyes, and said, "Yes, you do, Mrs. Shillstone."

"All right, then," she said. "Why don't you just meet me for breakfast in the morning?"

"We'll be getting up at first light."

"Meet me at the café," she said. "Bring the marshal. I just want to see you off."

"All right," he said. "The café, first light."

"And when you both get back from delivering the gold," she said, "we can talk about why I make you nervous."

Locke touched the brim of his hat and followed in Cooper's wake.

When he caught up to Cooper, his friend said, "I told you."

"Told me what?"

"She's got her eye on you."

"Nothing's going to happen, Coop."

"Why not? She's a mighty fine-lookin' woman."

"I told you," Locke said. "I'm not looking for a woman, fine-looking or otherwise."

"Not even just for the night?"

"Spending just one night with a woman like that wouldn't be smart," Locke said. "If that was what I wanted, I'd go to a saloon."

"Not in this town," Cooper said, shaking his head. "Believe me, I've seen the girls who work the saloons here. Not in this town."

Molly Shillstone knew she'd done a silly thing, inviting John Locke to her house. She didn't need to get mixed up with a man right now—especially not a man like him.

But there was something about John Locke. He was unlike any of the men in Turnback Creek—unlike any other man she'd ever met, in fact. It had been a while since she'd been with a real man, and the men who chased after her here in town, especially George Crowell, did not fit that description.

She stood on her porch, watching Locke and Cooper until they were out of sight, hugging herself against the chill in the air. No, it wasn't smart at all to show interest in Locke. From this point on, their relationship would be strictly business. That was the only way this whole thing was going to come out the way she wanted it to.

She turned and went back inside the house, closing the door firmly behind her.

NINETEEN

Robert Bailey met Hoke Benson and Eli Jordan at the livery stable, where they had saddled their horses and his.

"Well?" Hoke asked.

"They went back to shootin'," Bailey said. "Had some coffee at the café, talked to Molly Shillstone for a while, went to Hollaway's store, and then went back to shootin'."

"All right," Hoke said. "Mount up."

The plan was for the three of them to be in Kingdom Junction already when Cooper and Locke arrived. Hoke still hadn't decided where they would hit the payroll—at the railhead or on the trail—but he wanted to get a look at the layout before he decided.

"What about more men?" Bailey asked.

"I got a telegram back from the Junction," Hoke said. "There'll be two more men waitin' there for us."

"Do we know 'em?" Eli asked.

"I know 'em," Hoke said. "That's all that matters."

The three of them climbed astride their horses and started out of town. As they passed the hotel, they could hear the sound of gunfire emanating from behind it.

"A confident man don't have to practice with a gun," he told his two partners. "The fact that they're back there shootin' is good for us. They're both over the hill, boys."

"Maybe we didn't need to split the payroll with two other men, then," Eli said.

"There's plenty to go around," Hoke said. "Let's not start second-guessing ourselves. We'll stick to the plan."

"And what's the rest of the plan?" Bailey asked.

"I haven't decided yet," Hoke said. "But when I do, we'll stick to it."

TWENTY

Locke and Cooper didn't go back to shooting until they availed themselves of the line of credit Molly had arranged for them at the general store. After they outfitted themselves and made arrangements to pick up their supplies the next morning, they returned to their makeshift shooting gallery. Cooper seemed more relaxed and shot better, although not perfectly.

Holstering his gun, he said, "Maybe those days are gone. Maybe I need specs."

"Hey," Locke said, "even Hickok had eye problems."

Cooper finished reloading his gun and holstered it. "Like you said before," he commented, "maybe I'll shoot better the further I get from the bottle."

"How about some food?" Locke asked.

"You know," Cooper said, "just because I'm not drinkin' doesn't mean you can't go over to the saloon for a beer."

"I usually stick to one beer a day," Locke said.

"You used to drink a lot more than that, if I remember correctly," Cooper said.

"We have a lot more in common than you know, Coop," Locke told his friend.

"Like what?"

"Maybe when we're on the mountain, I'll tell you all about Tombstone."

They started walking down the alley back to the street.

"I heard you wore a badge in Tombstone," Cooper said. "It surprised me. You never were the type to wear a badge."

"That was the only time."

"Never again?"

"I never have since then," Locke said, "and I don't expect to again. It wasn't for me."

"The law isn't for everyone," Cooper said.

"You were always a great lawman, Coop."

"Yeah," Cooper said, "until Ellsworth."

"You know," Locke said, "Tombstone and Ellsworth are in our past. We should just keep moving forward."

"I don't know that I have much of a future left to me, John," Cooper said. "The West I knew is all but gone. Progress is not something I'm real comfortable with."

"Can't say I'm crazy about it, either," Locke said, "but what other choices do we have?"

Cooper hesitated, then said, "Maybe we can talk about that up on the mountain, too."

TWENTY-ONE

Locke and Cooper decided to put off eating. Cooper wanted to go back to his room for a while, and Locke had a sneaking suspicion the man wanted to see his landlady. Remembering that he still had to check out of the hotel and move his things to Mrs. Helms's rooming house, Locke told Cooper he'd be right along.

When Locke reached the rooming house and Mrs. Helms let him in, she said, "The marshal is having a nap."

"I'll be very quiet," he told her.

He took his things and put them in the room next to Cooper's, then found her waiting for him when he came back down.

"How did you do it?" she asked him.

"Do what?"

"How did you get him to stop drinking?" she asked. "I haven't known him very long, but I was so afraid that he was going to end up drinking himself to death."

"He simply told me he doesn't drink when he's working, ma'am," Locke said. "And now he's working."

"Taking that woman's payroll to her mine?"

"That's right." Locke wondered about the tone Ingrid Helms used when she said "that woman." "That's the job."

"And you're helping him?"

"Yes."

"Why?"

"Because he's my friend."

"If he's your friend, you should take him away from here."

"Why?"

"It doesn't matter how much that woman pays you," Ingrid said. "You're not doing the right thing."

"It's just a job, Mrs. Helms."

"For money?"

"Yes," he said. "But for Coop it's more. It's for self-respect."

"Foolish male pride," she said, shaking her head. "I've seen it so many times."

She turned and walked away from Locke without further word. Locke wondered what else she might have told him if he'd pushed her a bit further.

He turned and went out the front door. It was time for that one beer of the day.

Locke nursed his beer for a long time. He thought about Cooper and the change that had seemed to come over him in one day. He thought about Ingrid Helms and what she might have been wanting to tell him. And he thought about Molly Shillstone.

By far, the thing that occupied his mind the most was his friend, Dale Cooper. As dissatisfied as the old lawman had been with his own performance that day, Locke was amazed by it. How could there have been such a change in just one day?

He looked down at the remnants of his drink. He knew how long it had taken him to recover from his own drinking binges. Never had he undergone such a change in just one day.

Maybe up on the mountain, Cooper would tell him how he did it.

TWENTY-TWO

I n the morning, Locke and Cooper found Molly Shillstone waiting for them in the café.

"Good morning," she said. "I ordered steak and eggs
for all of us. I hope that's all right."

"It's fine," Cooper said. "I'm starving."

If Cooper had looked better after one day, he looked
ten times better after two.

Locke maneuvered himself around the table so he
could sit facing the front door. "How did you know when
we'd be here?" he asked. "Breakfast might have gotten
cold."

"You said you'd be up at first light," she said. "I simply
took you at your word."

The waiter came out, balancing three plates on his arm.
He set them on the table, paused to fill three cups with
coffee, and then withdrew.

"Are you gentlemen all ready?" Molly asked.

"We have to pick up some things at the general store," Cooper said, concentrating heavily on getting eggs and steak on his fork at the same time, "but we're ready. We just have to go to the livery and get our horses and then to your stable for the buckboard."

"I'm having someone hitch the team up as we eat," she said. "I arranged for it yesterday."

"Thank you," Cooper said. "That'll save us some time."

After breakfast they went outside together. Molly shook hands with both of them, holding onto Locke's a little longer.

"Good luck to both of you," she said. "I'll see you at Turnback Creek tomorrow afternoon."

"We'll be there," Locke said, sliding his hand free.

"If you're not, for some reason," she said, "I'll wait an extra day before panicking."

"Is there a telegraph office here in town?" he asked her.

"No," she said. "That's why I'll wait."

"If something goes wrong," Cooper said, "we'll try to get a message to you somehow."

"All right," she said.

They stepped from the boardwalk into the wet street and started walking toward the livery. It wasn't raining, but there was more in the offing, so they were carrying their slickers, along with their rifles.

"This is the day I've been waiting for," Cooper said. "The day we finally get started."

"We've got a lot of hard days ahead of us, Coop," Locke said. "Are you ready for it?"

Cooper looked at his friend. "Don't I look ready?"

He did. His eyes were clear, and there was a spring in his step that had not been there the day before. Any remnants of the man Locke had found unconscious in the Three Aces Saloon two days ago was gone.

"You look amazingly ready," Locke said.

"I feel like a young man again," Cooper said, "like ten or twelve years have melted away."

"I guess we'll see how young we both feel when we hit that mountain, Coop," Locke said. "A couple of duffers like us . . ."

"You're no duffer, John," Cooper said. "You're still a young man."

"I'm only six or seven years younger than you, Coop."

"Seems like more," Cooper said. "Sometimes it seems like there's a lifetime between you and me. I've always admired your strength, John. Did you know that?"

"I've always admired your courage, Coop," Locke said. "I guess we're both going to be put to the test in the next few days, huh?"

"More than you know, John," Cooper said. "More than you know."

TWENTY-THREE

Kingdom Junction was the largest town within a hundred-mile radius of Turnback Creek. What John Locke didn't know was whether the railroad had made it the biggest town or if it had already earned the title before that.

They rode past the train station on the way into town, saw that it was empty. No train, no people on the platform.

"What time's the train due?" Cooper asked Locke.

"What's it matter?" Locke asked. "It'll get here when it gets here. That's how trains are."

"So, what do we do in the meantime?" Cooper asked. "Kinda hard for us nondrinkers to pass the time, isn't it?"

"You just have to perfect new combinations."

"Like what?"

"Coffee and poker."

"In a saloon?"

"That's where you usually find poker."

Cooper looked at the empty platform again. He was driving the rig with his horse tied to the back of it.

"Okay," he said. "So, we're in the saloon, and the train pulls in. How do we know?"

"Come on, Coop," Locke said. "It's not like you never heard a train whistle before. They always blow it before they pull in. We'll hear it."

"You want to play poker that bad?"

"No," Locke said. "It's just a way to pass the time."

Cooper rubbed his hands over his lips.

"I tell you what," Locke said. "Forget the poker and the coffee. We'll go inside, ask about the train, and then hit the saloon. One cold beer each to wash down the dust, then we'll come back here and wait."

Cooper touched his mouth again and said, "Deal."

Cooper pulled the buckboard over, and Locke dismounted. They secured the horses and mounted the boardwalk to enter the station. There were empty wooden benches and a long wooden desk with a man standing behind it. "Help ya?" he asked.

"What time's the next train comin' in?" Cooper asked.

"Tomorrow."

"What?" Cooper snapped. "What do you mean, tomorrow? There's a train supposed to be comin' in today!"

The clerk narrowed his eyes and studied both Cooper and Locke. He was in his forties, kind of tired-looking, as if he'd either been up all night or got up real early that morning. "Are you the fella pickin' up Mrs. Shillstone's payroll?" he asked.

"Whaddaya know about that?" Cooper demanded.

The man shrugged and said, "Just that it's on the next train."

"Which was supposed to be in today, right?" Locke asked.

"That's right," the man said, "but they got engine trouble."

"So when are they getting in?" Cooper asked.

"Soon as they get another engine," the man replied, "or fix the one they got."

"Where are they now?" Locke asked, thinking that maybe they could go to wherever the train was now and pick up the gold.

"They're still in Kansas."

Locke shook his head. Too far for them to drive the buckboard.

"What's your best guess about when they'll be in?" he asked.

"Not before tomorrow, that's for sure," the man replied. "You fellas'd do well to get a hotel room for the night."

"Shit," Cooper said.

"You got a telegraph key here?"

"Sure do," the man said, pointing behind him. "That's how I know what's goin' on with the train."

"You mind if we check back with you later to see if you've got any more information?"

"I don't mind at all."

"Let's find a saloon," Locke said.

"Plenty of them in town."

"Say," Cooper said. "Who else knows about the payroll?"

"Beats me," the man said. "Ain't much of a secret, far as I kin tell."

"Okay," Locke said. "Much obliged."

They rode into town, found a saloon called Lucky Lil's, and pulled up in front of it. Locke tied off his horse, and Cooper hobbled the team. The streets were wet, but at the moment, it was not raining. There were black clouds in the sky, though.

"Two beers," Locke told the bartender before they even reached the bar. It was early, and the place was practically empty.

"Comin' up."

The place was small, with one faro table in a corner, covered for the day. The cover probably would come off around five o'clock. That wouldn't be for five more hours.

"Wasn't the train supposed to get in at noon?" Cooper asked the bartender.

"Train gets in when it gets in," the barman said. "Listen for the whistle."

Cooper looked at Locke, who shrugged. No point bellyaching about it anymore.

There were two tables occupied, one by two men who were nursing drinks and the other by three men playing poker for matchsticks. Not Locke's kind of game, even to pass the time.

He had drunk half his beer when he noticed that Cooper was finished with his and rubbing the back of his hand over his mouth. He quickly drained his mug and set it on the bar. "Lets go, Coop," he said.

"Look what they're doin'," Cooper said, pointing to the three men playing poker.

"For matchsticks," Locke said. "Not my game."

Cooper shook his head. Then he and Locke left the saloon.

"You want me to drive?" Locke asked.

"No," Cooper said, hoisting himself up in the seat of the buckboard. "We're just goin' to the damn livery. But you can drive when we leave here with the gold."

They figured the weight of the gold was going to double the time it took them to get there from Turnback Creek. Locke's butt probably would handle the trip better than Cooper's.

They pulled away from Lucky Lil's and headed over to the livery.

TWENTY-FOUR

"They looked right at us," Bailey said.

"Don't worry," Hoke said, studying his cards. "They don't know who we are."

"They might have seen us around Turnback Creek," Eli said.

"Relax, I said," Hoke replied. "I think I raised."

Eli and Bailey looked at their cards.

"Call," Bailey said.

"Call."

"You guys are too easy," Hoke said. He laid down three aces he'd been dealt.

"It's only damn matchsticks," Eli said, gathering up the cards for his next deal.

"You're never gonna learn that way," Hoke said.

"Hey," Bailey asked. "How are we supposed to know when the train comes in?"

"Didn't you hear what the bartender said?" Hoke

asked. "Listen for the whistle." He pushed his chair back and walked over to the other table, where Roy Turpin and Eddie Rome were sitting. "You see those two guys who came in?" he asked.

"Yep," Rome said.

"That was them."

"That Locke?" Turpin asked.

"Yeah, the younger one."

"I saw two old men," Turpin said.

"Shut up," Rome said. "When are we gonna hit 'em?"

"I'm still not sure," he said. "We'll trail 'em when they leave here, maybe hit 'em along the way, maybe not."

"Why not right at the station?" Turpin asked. "While they're loadin' the gold."

"I thought I told you to shut—" Rome started, but Hoke waved him off.

"It's okay," he said, then turned his attention to Turpin. "If we hit them here in town, the law will come runnin' when they hear shots. We've got to hit them along the trail or on the mountain. Understand?"

"I get it," Turpin said.

Hoke looked at Rome. "He gets it." He turned and went back to his poker game.

"Those guys gettin' antsy?" Eli asked.

Hoke sat back down. "Those guys are pros, Eli," Hoke said. "They don't get antsy—and neither should you."

He picked up his cards. Bailey had dealt him three kings. Some people are just lucky.

TWENTY-FIVE

Locke and Cooper left their horses and the buckboard at the livery and went out carrying their saddlebags and rifles. They stopped at the nearest hotel, the Gold Nugget, and got one room with two beds. They tossed their stuff on their beds, and Cooper sat down heavily.

"I don't like havin' to wait."

"Doesn't look like we have much of a choice, Coop," Locke said. "We can't do a damned thing until the train gets here."

"We're gonna have to let Molly know what's goin' on," Cooper said. "She's gonna be wonderin'."

"She'll be sitting out at the creek waiting for us," Locke said. "We better send someone back with a message. They can tell George, and then he can send someone to tell Molly."

"Sounds confusin'," Cooper said, rubbing his hand with his mouth.

"You want to stay here and rest up while I go and find someone to ride back?"

"Naw," Cooper said. "I'll go stir crazy sittin' here by myself. I'll come along with you."

"We might as well talk to the local law while we're at it, too," Locke said. "See what he knows."

"Why not?" Cooper asked. "If the whole town knows about the payroll, we oughta know about it."

Cooper got up from the bed, and the two men left the hotel. As they were walking out onto the street they saw a man crossing over toward them. The sun glinted off the badge he wore.

"Looks like we won't have to go looking for the sheriff," Locke said, inclining his head in the direction of the approaching lawman.

They stopped and waited, pretty sure that he was coming over to see the two of them.

"I'm Sheriff Maddox," the man said, stopping in front of them. His belly hung out over his gunbelt. "You the fellas from the Shillstone mine?"

"That's us, all right," Cooper said. "I'm Dale Cooper, and this here is John Locke."

"I know who you both are," the sheriff said. "Been waitin' for you to show up. Thought you'd check in with me."

"Matter of fact," Locke said, "that's just what we were on our way to do now."

"Looks like I saved you the trouble," Maddox said. "Some chairs right here. Let's set and talk a spell."

Locke turned and saw the wooden chairs in front of the hotel. There were five, and they each grabbed one.

"Guess you boys heard the train's gonna be late."

"We heard," Cooper said.

"We also heard some folks know about the payroll," Locke said.

"Heck fire, everybody in town knows about that," Maddox said. "Can't keep that much money a secret."

"How much money is that?" Locke asked.

"Well," Maddox said, rubbing his grizzled jaw, "I can't say as I know an exact number, but we heard it was a lot."

"What's your point?" Locke asked.

"Jest wanna put you boys on notice," Maddox said. "Somebody's gonna try to take that gold from ya."

"You sayin' you know who that somebody is?" Cooper asked.

"I ain't sayin' that at all," Maddox answered. "I'm just sayin' somebody's gonna try—they got to. You understand?"

"We understand," Cooper said.

"You ready to kill to protect that gold?" the lawman asked.

"That's what we're gettin' paid to do," Cooper said.

"Protecting the gold is our job," Locke added. "Not necessarily killing people."

"But you'll do it if you gotta?" Maddox asked.

"Let's just say we'll do what we have to do to get the job done," Locke replied.

"That's what I figured, from your reps."

"And what about you?" Cooper asked.

"What about me?"

"Are you ready to do what you gotta do?" Cooper asked. "Ready to do your job?"

"My job," Maddox said carefully, "is to keep the peace in this town. It ain't to help you protect your gold."

Locke didn't bother asking Maddox how he knew that the payroll was in gold. He decided to save that. "So, if someone tries to jump us for the payroll here in town, we can't count on your help?" he asked.

"That's kind of a blunt way of puttin' it," Maddox said, "but yeah, that's what I mean. I put my life on the line here for forty a month, but I ain't puttin' it on the line for somebody else's payroll."

Locke revised his opinion of the man. He looked fat and over the hill, but his eyes were intelligent, and he spoke like an educated man—except for the odd cadence.

"I guess that's clear enough," Cooper said. He looked at Locke, and they both stood up.

"Marshal, you got a rep as a lawman," Maddox said, "but you, Locke, yours is as a gunman. I don't want no trouble in my town, you hear? So don't be startin' any."

"I never start trouble, Marshal," Locke said, "but I usually finish it."

TWENTY-SIX

Bob Bailey came back into Lucky Lil's Saloon and sat down with Hoke Benson and Eli Jordan, who were still playing poker for matchsticks. Eddie Rome and Roy Turpin were still sitting together at their table, staring into space over their beers. Several other tables were in use now, and there were a few men standing at the bar. The tables were still covered, and no dealers or girls had appeared yet.

"What?" Hoke asked.

"They got a hotel room."

"What for?" Eli asked.

"I wondered that myself," Bailey said, "so I went to the railroad station and asked after the train." Both men stopped playing cards and stared at Bailey. "What?"

"You went and did that on your own?" Eli asked.

"Without havin' to be told?" Hoke asked.

"Why not?" Bailey asked. "I ain't stupid, you know."

Truth of the matter was, Bailey knew that if he went back to the saloon without checking on the train, Hoke would have sent him to do just that. This way, he figured he saved himself a trip.

"Okay," Hoke said. "What did you find out at the station?"

Bailey told Hoke about the train being late and probably not arriving until tomorrow.

"What do you think we should do?" he asked after he'd finished explaining.

"What can we do?" Hoke said. "We got to wait."

"Get some matchsticks, Bob," Eli said. "We're gonna be here awhile."

While Bailey went to the bar to get some more matchsticks and a beer, Hoke got up and walked over to where Rome and Turpin were sitting. He told them about the change of plan.

"I don't care if we sit here for days," Rome said, "as long as that pot of gold is at the end of the rainbow."

"What rainbow?" Turpin asked.

Hoke and Eddie Rome ignored him.

"You sure you don't want to hit them now?" Rome asked.

"They don't even have the gold yet."

Rome shrugged and said, "We hit them, and then we collect the gold from the train."

"They gotta have some kind of paper to show the guards on the train," Hoke said.

"We grab that, too."

"No," Hoke said. "They already talked to the local law. We'd never pull that off."

"Okay," Rome said. "You're callin' the play. We'll sit here and wait."

"You wanna come over and play poker?" Hoke asked.

"What's the stakes?" Turpin asked.

"Matchsticks."

"Matchsticks?" Turpin said. "What the hell am I gonna do with matchsticks?"

"Light cigarettes," Hoke said.

"I don't even smoke."

"Okay," Hoke said. "Forget it."

"We'll be fine over here," Rome said.

Hoke nodded and went back to his table.

Both Rome and Turpin waited for Hoke to reach his table and sit down with his companions before speaking.

"What are we gonna do?" Turpin asked Rome.

"We'll wait."

"We still gonna take the gold away from those three?"

"First chance we get," Rome said. "It'll be easy."

"And there'll be a heckuva lot more with just a two-way split," Turpin said.

"Yeah," Rome said, staring at Turpin. "A lot more."

And a lot more, he thought, *with a one-way split, too.*

TWENTY-SEVEN

Locke and Cooper each picked a bench on the railroad platform. The ex-marshal had wanted to go to a saloon, but Locke wanted to keep him away from temptation, so he suggested they go and sit at the station. Cooper rolled two cigarettes and handed one to Locke first.

"We still got to find somebody to ride to Turnback Creek with the news," he said. "We're only gonna find someone for that at the saloon."

"Or the livery."

Cooper looked at Locke. "I suppose you think I should go to the livery and you should go to the saloon, eh?"

"Coop—"

"No, no, that's okay," Cooper said. "I understand you feeling that way. I guess I'd feel like that if—"

"Coop," Locke said, cutting him off, "I was going to say we'll go together. We just need some young fella with a horse who wants to make himself a few dollars."

"That shouldn't be too hard."

Both men stared off down the tracks, as if trying to will the train into view. It wasn't working.

"Tell me, what would you do with this much gold?" the ex-marshal suddenly asked.

"What?" Locke wasn't sure he'd heard right.

"The gold," Cooper said. "If you had it all, what would you do with it? How would you spend it?"

"Why are you asking me that?"

Cooper shrugged. "I'm just making conversation."

Instead of answering the question, Locke turned it back on his friend. "What would you do with it, Coop?"

"I'd buy myself a ranch in Mexico," Cooper said without hesitation, "and a *señorita* to go with it. Oh, not a young girl. I'd look silly with a young girl. Maybe a woman of about forty."

"It sounds like you've given the question a lot of thought, Coop," Locke said.

Cooper shrugged and said, "Like I said, I'm just passin' the time."

"Let's pass it talking about something else," Locke said.

"You don't wanna answer?"

"I don't indulge in those kinds of fantasies."

"Then answer me this," Cooper said. "The men who robbed the first payroll, you think they'd stay around to try for the second one?"

"Why not?" Locke asked. "They'd have to know that Molly had to replace it. And if they hung around town, they'd know how the miners felt. They'd know she was doing more than just replacing the payroll that was stolen. Oh, yeah, I'd hang around."

TWENTY-EIGHT

Cal Nieves opened the door of the general store and let Del Morgan in. Del worked at the livery stable. Cal worked at the general store for the owner, Arthur Koble.

"Come on in," Cal said. "Everybody else is here."

"Good," Morgan said. "Where are they?"

"Back room."

The two men crossed the store and entered the back storeroom. There were three more men waiting there. All, like Morgan and Nieves, were in their late twenties. It was because they were close in age that they were friends. They had grown up together, and while the town was prospering with age, they were not. They all had menial jobs around town, like Cal Nieves's clerking job at the general store.

"Hello, boys," Morgan said.

"Del," Clete Cloninger said, "what the hell is this

about? Why are we meetin' secretly behind the store here?"

"Yeah," Malcolm Turner said. "What gives?"

The fifth man was Red Sinclair, and he was, as usual, a man of few words. He let people know his mood with a look, and his look was clouded at the moment.

"Take it easy, fellas," Morgan said. "Hear me out. Now, we've all heard about this payroll that's comin' into town on the next train, right?"

"Right," Cloninger said. "The Shillstone payroll. So what?"

"It's in gold," Morgan said.

Turner said, "We know that, too. What the hell does that have to do with us, Del?"

Morgan looked at each man in turn and said, "We're gonna steal it."

"We're gonna what?" Cloninger demanded.

"Who's we?" Turner asked. "Who made this decision?"

"Cal and I have been talkin' about it," Morgan said, "and we decided to cut you in."

"Well, that's real nice of you boys," Cloninger said, "to cut us in on a harebrained scheme that's bound to get us killed!" He stood up. "Let's go, Malcolm."

As he and Turner stood up, Red Sinclair—the biggest man in the room, by far— stepped in their way.

"See?" Morgan said. "Red wants to hear the rest."

"Well, Red can stay if he likes," Cloninger said. "We're leavin'."

"I don't think so, Cletus," Morgan said. "I think Red wants you and Malcolm to stay and hear the rest."

"Get out of my way, Red—" Cloninger started, but he was cut off by Nieves.

"Oh, what the hell is the harm in hearin' us out, Clete?" he demanded. "Besides, do you really want to get Red mad?"

Cloninger looked into the face of the six-foot-six man who was blocking his path.

"Cletus," Turner said, "I don't wanna get Red mad."

Cloninger exchanged a glance with Turner, then whipped around and said, "Fine. We'll listen."

"Good," Morgan said. "Here's what Cal and I propose . . ."

When Morgan was finished with his proposal, Cloninger said, "What about the sheriff?"

"He's not gonna be involved."

"But Del," Turner said, "the Widowmaker? And an ex-marshal?"

"An over-the-hill marshal," Morgan said. "I heard from someone who passed through Turnback Creek that this ex-lawman, Dale Cooper, is a hopeless drunk."

"And what about the Widowmaker?"

"What about him?" Morgan asked. "I got a look at him today. He's only one man, and he ain't that far from bein' the marshal's age himself. I tell you boys, we can do this."

"How much money is involved?" Turner asked.

"We're not real sure," Morgan said, "but I hear tell Molly Shillstone is bringin' in more than the miners got comin', 'cause she don't want them walkin' out on her."

"It's a lot of money, Cletus," Nieves said, "and it's in gold."

"Gonna be heavy," Turner said.

"That's why we're gonna take their buckboard, too," Morgan said, "and that's why we got Red."

Cloninger and Turner looked at Sinclair, who was staring straight ahead at Morgan.

"I think Red is in, boys," Morgan said. "What about you?"

"Are we gonna have to k-kill anybody?" Turner asked.

"They're just two old men, Malcolm," Morgan said. "All we probably have to do is show them our guns, and they'll give us the gold. They ain't gonna want to die for it."

Turner looked at Cloninger.

"Come on, Malcolm," Morgan said. "Make up your own mind, for once. Do you want to work in a hardware store all your life?"

Turner looked at Morgan and then at Nieves.

"Okay," he said nervously. "I'm in."

"That only leaves you, Cletus," Morgan said. "What do you say? Do you want to be a rich man?"

" 'Course I do."

"You think you're gonna get rich bein' a clerk in city hall?"

Morgan thought about it for a few minutes, then he said, "No, by God, I don't. I'm in."

A huge hand fell onto his shoulder, and when he turned and looked at Red Sinclair, the big man was smiling.

TWENTY-NINE

Locke and Cooper left the train station after checking with the clerk to see if he had any further news on the train.

"Last I heard, they thought they were gonna be able to fix the engine," said Fred Dooley, the clerk. "She should be here late tomorrow."

"Late?"

"That's right."

"Two more nights in the hotel," Locke said to Cooper as they walked away from the station.

"Goddamnit!" Cooper said. "We're gonna be sittin' targets if we can't leave as soon as the gold gets here."

"We'll have to stay up with it all night," Locke said. "Sleep in the buckboard, and take turns standing watch. We'll need an enclosed space."

"The livery."

"Right," Locke said. "Let's go over there. Maybe we can rent a space and find a messenger at the same time."

When they reached the livery, they found a man mucking out the stalls by himself.

"Help ya?" He was a large man, heavy through the shoulders and chest, about forty or so. He put the harmless end of his pitchfork on the ground and faced them.

"My name is Dale Cooper, and this is John Locke," Cooper started. "We're here from—"

"The Shillstone mine," the man said. "You're here to pick up the payroll from the train, right?"

"Does everyone know about the payroll?" Locke asked.

"Just about," the man said. "My name's Ed Milty. What can I do for you fellas?"

"We need two things," Locke said, and went on to explain just what they were.

"Well, you can rent the whole place overnight if you want," Milty said. "I'd be closed anyway. As for the messenger, my boy can do it."

"How old is he?"

"Sixteen."

"You trust him to ride to Turnback Creek?" Locke asked.

"He's done it before," Milty said. "He's a good kid, responsible. You can trust him to deliver your message."

"What's his name?" Cooper asked.

"Frank."

"We're at the Gold Nugget Hotel," Locke said. "Have him come over there. We'll be sitting out front."

"You got it," Milty said. "He'll be over in about ten minutes."

"Now," Locke said, "about the cost of renting this place for the night . . ."

Frank Milty turned out to be a big sixteen-year-old who, when he filled out, would obviously be built like his father. By the time he got to the hotel, where Locke and Cooper were sitting out front, they had written out a note for him to deliver.

"Do you know where the Shillstone mine office is?" Locke asked.

"Yes, sir."

"Deliver this to a man named George Crowell, and wait for an answer," Cooper said, handing the boy the note.

"Don't fool around over there, boy," Locke said. "Come right back, and there's another two dollars in it for you." Locke handed the boy two dollars.

"Yes, sir!"

The boy went running off to get his horse.

"Two dollars?" Cooper asked. "I was gonna give him two bits."

"I'm a bigger spender than you are."

"Obviously."

Locke took his hat, smoothed his hair back, and replaced the hat. He sat back in his chair so that the back was against the wall and the front legs were just up off the boardwalk.

"So, what do we do now?" Cooper asked.

"We wait."

"Be easier to wait with a drink."

"Just one?"

Cooper rubbed his face vigorously. "No," he said. "One wouldn't do it."

"There must be some other way to occupy your time in this town," Locke said.

"Like what?"

"Is whiskey the only thing you like?" Locke asked. "What about women?"

"At my age?"

"Jesus," Locke said. "You're not dead, Coop. Go over to the local cathouse, pick out a young pretty whore, and see what you can do."

Cooper sat there for a few moments, thinking it over, then said, "Goddamnit, you're right. Why not? I'll do it." He stood up. "You comin' along?"

"I'm happy just sitting right here and relaxing," Locke said. "This might be the last chance I get."

"I'll be back," Cooper said, "hopefully later than sooner."

Locke hoped it would be later, too.

THIRTY

Pretty Polly's was the local whorehouse. Polly Kennelly ran it, and she was anything but. In her younger days, she had been very pretty, but those days were gone. She was thirty years and sixty pounds from ever being Pretty Polly again.

She had some pretty girls in her house, though, all shapes and sizes and colors.

"What's your pleasure?" she asked Bob Bailey. He'd decided to while away some time with a whore, since the train wasn't going to be coming in for a day or so. Playing poker for matchsticks wasn't his idea of a good time.

"Black?" Polly asked. "Yellow? Skinny, fat? I got 'em all. You won't find a better selection of girls at the best whorehouse in San Francisco."

Bailey didn't know about that. He'd never been to San Francisco, but he hoped to get there after they grabbed this second payroll.

The girls were lined up in front of him, and he spotted one he liked. He'd never been with a Chinese gal before. This one was petite, but he could see the dark circles of her nipples through the filmy nightie she was wearing.

"The Chinee," he said.

"Ah, good choice," Polly said. "That's Lotus. She knows things none of the other girls know. Brought them over with her from the Orient."

Bailey didn't care where she came from.

"Lotus, would you take the nice gentleman up to your room, and please show him a good time?"

The girl approached him and took his hand in her tiny one. She barely came to his shoulder, and when she smiled up at him, he felt it in his loins.

"You come," she said, tugging his hand. "I make you vellee hoppy."

Polly watched them go up the stairs. She knew that the phony accent Lotus used got to a lot of men, and this one seemed no different.

Twenty minutes later, Dale Cooper walked in, and Polly greeted him with the same patter.

Black?

Yellow?

Fat?

Skinny?

Blond?

Brunet?

Young?

Old?

She got through the entire list before Cooper pointed to a girl.

"That one."

She was blond, in her thirties, older than the others. Cooper decided he would have felt silly picking one of the young ones.

"Ah," Polly said. "The one thing I didn't ask about—experience. Yes, Jill is one of our most experienced girls. She knows things none of the others know. Jill, would you take the gentleman up to your room and show him a good time, please?"

"Of course," Jill said, coming forward and taking Cooper's hand. She had large, round breasts, and Cooper could plainly see them through her gauzy top. She was not as slender as most of the other girls, but that worked in her favor, as far as Cooper was concerned. He liked women with some extra flesh on them.

As she led the way up the stairs, he smelled her perfume and watched her fleshy buttocks twitch in front of him and was happy to feel something stirring. Apparently, his friend John Locke was right. He wasn't dead.

Lotus took Bob Bailey to room number three. After they entered, she said, "Put money on the dresser, prease?"

Bailey dug the bills out of his pocket and put them on the table, all crumpled.

"Now you sit," she said. "I wash."

He thought she meant she was going to wash herself, but she took off his shoes and his trousers and his underwear and proceeded to use a wash cloth and basin to wash him. By the time she was done, he was erect and almost ready to pop.

"You very big," she said, stroking him.

"Jesus," he said, and closed his eyes . . .

Jill took Dale Cooper to room number four.

"Could you please put the money on the table?" she asked. "I like to get that out of the way first."

"Sure," he said.

He took the bills from his pocket, smoothed them out, and put them on the dresser.

"Now, if you'll remove your clothes, I can wash you," she said. "We like to make sure our customers are clean."

"Sure, sure," he said, "I understand."

He pulled off his boots, then stood up to remove his trousers and long underwear, almost tripping in the process.

"Hey," she said, bringing a basin of water and a cloth over to the bed. "Are you nervous, handsome?"

"A little," he admitted, sitting on the bed.

"Don't be," she said, getting on her knees in front of him. "Everything will be fine."

She used the cloth to wash him, and by the time she was done, he was happy to see that he was still capable.

"Now," she said, sitting back on her heels and letting her nightie fall from her shoulders. Her breasts were big and firm, with pale, smooth skin and pink nipples. "What would you like? Do you like French, or would you prefer straight fucking?"

"Uh, I'm not sure what that means, French," he admitted.

"Well," she said, leaning forward and sliding her hands up his thighs, "let me show you . . ."

"Is okay," Lotus said to an embarrassed Bob Bailey. "It happens to many men."

Bailey was getting dressed and was inconsolable. He hadn't even gotten the Chinese girl on the bed. He was convinced that she'd teased him with the washing and had gotten him to the point where he couldn't stop himself. His embarrassment was quickly turning to anger.

"Just forget it," he snapped.

"Come, you stay," she said, reaching for him. "Next time, you last longer, I promise."

"Ain't gonna be a next time," he said. "Not with you." He walked to the dresser and grabbed his money.

"Hey," she said, dropping her accent. "My money!"

He glared at her and said, "You talk real English!"

"You can't take my money!"

"I oughta take some of your hide, girl," he said. "Yer nothin' but a damn tease."

"Hey," she said. "You got your nut—don't you hit me!" She shrank back from him.

"I ain't gonna waste no time hittin' you," he said, stuffing his money back into his pocket.

But as he turned to head for the door, she overcame her fear and gave in to her own anger at losing her money and jumped on his back.

"Bitch!" he shouted. He tried to get her off, and when

he couldn't, he rushed backward until he slammed her into the wall between rooms three and four.

Cooper was right in the middle of learning what French meant when there was a loud thud on the wall, and then a woman began screaming for help.

"What the—" he said.

Jill released him and said, "That's Lotus's room."

The screaming and banging were becoming more and more intense, until it sounded as if they were going to crash through the wall.

"Somebody's gotta help her!" Jill said, jumping to her feet and running for the door.

"Damn!" Cooper said. The place must have had a bouncer, but it might take him time to get up the stairs. His long johns were pooled at his feet, so he pulled them on, grabbed his gun, and ran out the door after Jill.

THIRTY-ONE

Locke saw the lawman walking purposefully toward the hotel and wondered if he was once again coming to see him.

"You wanna come with me?" Sheriff Maddox asked.

"Why?"

"When I told you boys to stay out of trouble, I thought it would be you I'd have to deal with."

Locke stood up. "What are you talking about?"

"Your partner got himself into trouble over at Pretty Polly's," Maddox said. "Our local cathouse."

"Where is he now?"

"In a cell. You comin'?"

Locke stepped down off the boardwalk and followed the sheriff to his office.

"You ever heard of French?" Cooper asked.

"What?"

"You know," Cooper said. "French."

"You mean, like . . . the language?"

"No," Cooper said. "I mean what a whore does to you. They call it French, or Frenchin'."

"No, Coop," Locke said. "I've never heard of it."

"You should try it," Cooper said. "It's really nice."

"Is that what this is about?" Locke asked him through the bars. "Some whore Frenching you?"

"No," Cooper said. "It's about what happened that interrupted her while she was . . . doin' it to me."

"I guess you're gonna have to explain this to me."

At that moment, though, Sheriff Maddox came walking into the cell block with his keys.

"You're free to go, Cooper."

"What?" Locke asked.

He stepped back from the cell so Maddox could unlock the door. They both followed him into his office, where he laid Cooper's hat and gun and gun belt on his desk.

"Polly ain't pressin' charges, and neither is the man you cold-cocked. In fact, Polly says to tell you that you got a freebie comin'."

"Damn right, I should have," Cooper said, collecting his belongings, "since I didn't even get what I paid for."

"Who did he cold-cock?"

"Some cowboy who was havin' a dispute with his whore."

"Don't they have bouncers for that?" Locke asked, looking at Cooper.

"Sure they do, but my whore went runnin' out the door," he said. "I didn't want nothin' to happen to her."

"So, what did happen?"

"I followed her into the next room and found her and the other whore both strugglin' with this cowboy."

"So?"

"So, I clubbed him with the butt of my gun. He went down, and somebody called the sheriff."

"That sounds about right," Maddox said.

"Then what was he doing in a locked cell in the first place?" Locke demanded.

"I had to get the story straight," Maddox argued. "It didn't do him no harm to spend an hour in a cell."

"And where's the other fella?" Locke asked.

"He was at the doc's. Cooper here opened up his skull some."

"He was tryin' to get out of the whorehouse without payin'," Cooper said. "He was gonna hurt that girl."

"That wasn't your affair, Cooper," Maddox said. "You ain't a lawman anymore."

Cooper grumbled and strapped on his gun.

"Come on, Coop," Locke said. "Let's get out of here."

Down the street, Hoke Benson was leaving the doctor's office with Bob Bailey.

"I can't let you go anywhere without getting into trouble, can I?" he demanded.

"It wasn't my fault!" Bailey whined. "That marshal clubbed me when I wasn't lookin'. Why are you makin' me drop the charges?"

"Because, moron," Hoke said, "we need that marshal to be out of jail to collect the gold."

"Well, with him in jail, Locke would have to get it himself, wouldn't he?" Bailey asked.

"No," Hoke said. "He'd get some help, somebody younger and in better shape than that old man. Jesus, it's a good thing we don't depend on you for any thinkin'!"

Hoke tapped Bailey's head, and the man cried out. His hat was sitting funny on top of the bandage the doctor had applied after stitching him up.

"Jesus," Hoke said. "You're too stupid for words, Bob. Come on."

"Where?"

"Back to the saloon, where at least I can keep an eye on you."

On their way to the saloon, they saw Locke and Cooper coming out of the sheriff's office.

"Don't even look across the street," Hoke warned Bailey. "I don't want them getting a good look at us."

Despite the warning, Bailey tossed a glare across at Dale Cooper, who returned it in kind.

"Aren't those two of the men who were playing poker for matchsticks in Lucky Lil's?" Locke asked.

"Huh?"

"Coop!"

Cooper pulled his gaze away from the man across the street and looked at Locke.

"The matchstick poker game," Locke said again. "Is that them?"

"I think so," Cooper said. "What if it is?"

"I don't know," Locke said. "They just seem to be sitting around killing time."

"Like we are?" Cooper asked.

"Yes, as a matter of fact," Locke said. "Just like we are."

THIRTY-TWO

"What are you sayin'?" Cooper asked. "That those matchstick-playin' fools are after the gold?"

"Could be," Locke said. "Do you remember seeing them in Turnback Creek?"

Cooper thought for a moment, then said, "Can't say that I do. What about you?"

"I'm trying to," Locke said.

"Maybe we better just keep an eye on them."

"No," Locke said. "Not when you've already had a run-in with one of them. Let's just keep an eye out for them."

"There could be dozens of men plannin' to try for that gold, John," Cooper said. "I don't think that men who play poker for matchsticks are gonna be much of a danger."

"You never know."

They were in a café they found off the main street, having some dinner. Cooper was trying to shake off the feeling of being behind bars. He told Locke it had never happened before—not with the door locked—and he didn't like it one bit.

"I'll tell you one thing," Cooper said.

"What's that?"

"Anybody tryin' to steal that gold better be ready to die," the older man said, " 'cause I ain't gonna stand for it."

"You sound like you're taking this pretty personal, Coop."

"I'm takin' it damn personal."

"Why is that?"

"Huh?"

"Why are you taking it so personally?" Locke asked again. "It's not our gold."

"Well . . . we're bein' paid to protect it and deliver it," Cooper said. "That makes it more my gold than anybody who tries to steal it."

Locke ate the last piece of his steak and pushed the plate away without finishing the vegetables.

"You not gonna eat those?" Cooper asked.

"No," Locke said. "Some are soggy, and others are hard. I don't know how they managed to overcook and undercook something at the same time."

"I'll take 'em."

Cooper grabbed Locke's plate and scraped it off onto his own.

"Looks like your appetite has come back," Locke said.

"Hmm? Oh, yeah," Cooper said. "Maybe it's got somethin' to do with bein' in jail."

"You think so?" Locke asked. "Could be, I guess."

He watched his old friend demolish what was on his

plate and then grab the last biscuit from the basket on the table. He sure didn't look like a man with only whiskey on his mind.

Locke didn't know what he was going to do after dinner. It was too early to turn in. Normally, he'd kill a lot of time in the saloon, nursing the one beer he drank a day and—if the place was large enough—watching some gambling. Might even go upstairs with some likely-looking saloon girl. But he was worried about what Cooper would do if he left him alone. While he didn't look as if he was craving liquor at the moment, Locke knew for a fact that a craving like that could come on at any moment.

"So, what do we do now?" Cooper asked, pushing away his plate and touching his belly with satisfaction.

"I don't know, Coop."

"Oh, for Chrissake, John," Cooper said. "Normally, you'd go to the saloon and have a beer after dinner, wouldn't ya?"

"Well . . . yeah, I would."

"Then go have one," Cooper said. "I'll go back to the room and clean my guns or somethin'."

"Are you sure?"

"I'm positive . . . and don't be thinkin' I'm gonna sneak out to some other saloon," the ex-marshal said. "I know I got to be straight for what we got to do here. Just don't worry about me."

"Okay," Locke said. "I won't. Maybe you can go on over to the whorehouse and get your freebie."

As they got up and left the money on the table for their check, Cooper said, "I got in trouble once already goin' over there. Think I'll just do like I said and go back to the room."

They left the café and stopped just outside.

"I think I'll stop over at the train station before going to the saloon," Locke said.

"I'll see you back at the room, then."

The two men parted company and went their separate ways. Locke hoped that Cooper would be true to his word and stay in the room. He decided not to spy on the man but to take him at his word and be done with it. As he walked over to the rail station, he tried to put his old friend's drinking out of his head.

"They're under way," the clerk said as Locke entered the station. "That was the last word I got. They should be here sometime tomorrow afternoon."

"That's good news," Locke said. Depending on how late in the afternoon, though, they still might have to spend another night in town. That night would be spent in the livery, guarding the gold.

Locke left the train station and headed over to Lucky Lil's to have his beer.

THIRTY-THREE

"Don't look at him," Hoke said to Bailey when Locke entered the saloon. "I don't want it to look like we're interested in him."

The saloon was in full swing now, gaming tables uncovered, girls working the room, all the tables taken.

"It's the other one I want," Bailey said. "The old man." He put his hand to his head, where his hat was still sitting askew atop the bandages.

"You'll get your chance, Bob," Hoke said. "Just be patient, and don't pay Locke any mind. You got that, Eli?"

"I got it," Eli said. "I raise ten matchsticks."

As Locke entered, he noticed that the three men were still playing poker for matchsticks, while everyone else in the room who was gambling was doing so with real money. That made the three men an oddity, and they were drawing attention for it.

He walked to the bar, elbowed his way to it, and ordered his only beer for the day. Conversation on either side of him seemed to be about the men playing poker for matchsticks.

"They sure are concentratin' like they was playin' for real money," someone said.

Locke noticed that they were concentrating very hard, especially the man with the bandage on his head. They had seen Locke with Cooper, and he wondered if the man Cooper had clubbed had orders not to look up.

Locke decided to see just how hard the men could continue to concentrate. He turned his back so he could nurse his beer and watch the three men at the same time.

"He's starin' at us," Bailey said.

"So what?" Hoke said. "Let him stare. Everybody else is."

"They're starin' 'cause of this bandage on my head."

"You idiot," Eli said. "They're starin' because we're playin' poker with matchsticks!"

"Look," Hoke said impatiently. "It don't matter why anybody is starin'. Just play your damn cards."

"But what if he knows—" Bailey started.

"Knows what?" Hoke asked. "What could he know? That we're waitin' to steal the payroll? Hell, I bet there's a dozen men in here makin' plans for that payroll."

"We ain't gonna let nobody else take it, are we, Hoke?" Bailey asked anxiously.

"Nobody's takin' that payroll, Bob," Hoke said. "It's ours. Now, just play."

* * *

"What the hell are they doin'?" Turpin asked Rome.

"They're killin' time, Roy," Rome said. "That's all."

"Everybody's lookin' at them."

"Yeah, well," Rome said, "that's their problem, ain't it? You relax and drink your beer. Maybe take one of the girls upstairs. Don't worry about what they're doin'."

Turpin eyed a blonde who was walking by at that moment and said, "You know, I just might do that."

Locke continued to watch the three men play cards, while others eventually tired of it and turned their attention to other things. A blond saloon girl came up to him and stood in front of him. She sucked in her tummy and stuck out her impressive chest and smiled. Her breasts were almost balloonlike and incredibly pale. She succeeded in attracting his attention away from the three men because of her pretty face and impressive physique.

"My name is Katy," she said. "Do you see anything you like?"

"Quite a bit," he said. It was hard not to see quite a bit, since she was showing almost all she had.

"Can I interest you in a trip upstairs?" she asked.

He looked down at the inch of beer remaining in his mug and considered it. What else did he really have to do except stare at the three men? It had been a long time between women for him—and a long time since he had one who looked like this.

"Why not?" he said. He tossed off the rest of the beer,

put his arm around her shoulders, and walked upstairs with her.

Katy wasted no time once they were in her room. She divested herself of her clothing, revealing her opulence in all its glory. She was more than a handful everywhere he looked and touched, her flesh pliant and warm, her mouth eager and wet.

She undressed him slowly, and he was just hanging his gun belt on the bedpost when the door was kicked open and two men rushed into the room, guns in hand.

Locke pushed Katy away, hoping to get her out of the line of fire, and drew his gun from his holster. The two men fired as he was moving, and their shots went into the wall and the pillows. As he hit the floor, he fired three times in quick succession, and it was by dint of his experience and reflexes that all three shots struck home.

One man dropped like a stone, while the other—hit twice—was propelled out the door and into the hall.

Locke got to his feet quickly and moved to the first man. He kicked the man's fallen gun across the room, then leaned over to see if he was dead. Satisfied that he was, he stepped out into the hall, where doors had opened, people were peering out, and others were coming up the stairs from the saloon. He kicked the man's gun down the hall, leaned over, and made doubly sure he was dead. Unmindful of the fact that he was naked and still semi-tumescent, he called out, "Somebody get the sheriff."

He turned to go back into his room and found that a woman in the room across from him was peeking out, taking in his nude form with unabashed admiration. Behind her on her bed was a naked fat man with whom she had been doing business.

"Ma'am," he said, and stepped back into the room.

He looked around for Katy and found her on the floor. Apparently, he hadn't shoved her far enough away from the action, or someone's shot had gone wild. Either way, a bullet had perforated her opulent flesh, and her blood was starkly red in contrast to her pale skin.

Since he didn't know yet if she had set him up or was an innocent victim, he reserved feeling sorry for her until he found out for sure. He gathered up his clothes and got dressed to meet with Sheriff Maddox, who was not going to be happy.

THIRTY-FOUR

"I'm not happy, Locke!" Maddox said.

The hall had been cleared of people, and Maddox had several men from the saloon remove the bodies of the men. Katy's body was still on the floor of her room.

"I'm not real happy about this, either, Sheriff," Locke said.

"You think the girl was in on it?" Maddox asked.

"Sheriff," Locke said, "I'm not even sure what 'it' was. This could have been two men trying to make a name for themselves, or it could have been about the payroll."

"You don't even have the payroll yet."

"Maybe they figured Cooper would have to collect it alone, and he'd be easier pickings without me."

"Well, I don't know either one of those men," the lawman said. "They're not local. My bet would be they recognized you and wanted to make a name."

"And the girl?"

Maddox rubbed his jaw and stared down at her.

"Katy sure was something, wasn't she?" he asked.

"I never quite found out."

After they'd removed Katy's body, they found fifty dollars secreted in her dress. Since Locke had not given her any money, both he and the sheriff assumed that the two men had paid her to lure Locke up to her room.

"Maybe," Maddox said across his desk, "she didn't know they were going to kill you."

Sitting opposite him, Locke said, "Or that they'd end up killing her, actually."

"You don't think a shot from your gun might have done it?"

"I fired three times," Locke said. "Check the bodies before you start measuring me for a cell."

"I should put you in a cell, just for your own good," Maddox said. "Your friend, too."

"Shit," Locke said, jumping to his feet.

"What?"

"If this was about the payroll, somebody will probably try for Cooper, too," Locke said.

"Hey, wait—" Maddox said, but Locke had already gone out the door on the run. Maddox sighed, got up, and followed at a more sedate pace.

Locke got to the hotel and found it quiet and peaceful. The desk clerk looked up at him as he burst through the door.

"Is something wrong, sir?"

"Has anyone come in here in the past half hour?"

"No, sir," the young clerk said. "No one."

"You have a back door?"

"Yes, sir, but it's kept locked."

"Check it for me, will you?"

"Well . . . of course."

While Locke was waiting for the clerk to return, the sheriff entered the lobby behind him.

"Looks quiet."

"I'm having the clerk check the back door."

"Why don't you go up and check on Cooper?" Maddox said. "I'll wait for the clerk."

"Good idea."

Locke went upstairs and found the hall as quiet as the lobby. He went to his door and opened it with the key.

"Coop, something happened that—"

He stopped short when he realized the room was empty.

"Damn it, Coop!"

THIRTY-FIVE

When Locke got to the lobby, Maddox was waiting with the clerk, leaning on the desk.

"Well?" Maddox asked. "Did you wake the old boy up?"

"The old boy's not in the room," Locke said.

"Maybe he went back to the whorehouse," the lawman said. "I better get over there and see if he's causing any more trouble."

"He didn't cause trouble the first time," Locke said, "but go ahead, suit yourself."

"What are you gonna do?"

"I'll check the other saloons in town."

"There's three more," Maddox said, "but none as big as Lucky Lil's."

"I just hope he stayed away from there," Locke said. "That fella he cold-cocked is there with his friends."

"I'll check there, too," Maddox said.

"Okay, thanks."

"Come by my office in a little while," Maddox said, "and we'll see who found him."

"Thanks."

Locke didn't have long to look. The first saloon he stopped in was a little place called Little Annie's. Idly, he wondered why all the saloons in town seemed to be named after women.

Cooper was sitting at a table in the all but empty saloon, staring down at a glass of whiskey. There was only one other man in the place, and he had his head down on the table, much the way Locke had first found Cooper in Turnback Creek.

Locke walked over and sat down opposite Cooper.

"Hey, John," Cooper said without looking up.

"Coop."

"In case you're wonderin'," the older man said, "this is the first one I ordered."

"You didn't drink it."

"No."

"Not yet?"

Cooper looked up from the drink and at his friend. "No, not at all. I was going to, though. I thought I could come out, have one, and go back to the room, and you'd never know."

"So, what stopped you?"

Cooper reached down and pushed the whiskey over to Locke's side of the table.

"I knew if I drank this one, I wouldn't be able to stop."

"That's good, Coop," Locke said. "That's real good."

"Yeah."

Both men stared at the whiskey, and then Locke picked it up, carried it over to the other occupied table, and put it down next to the slumbering man. It would be a nice surprise for him when he woke up.

"I heard some commotion," Cooper said when Locke returned.

"Yeah, that was me," Locke said. "Come on, I'll tell you about it on the way back to the hotel . . ."

Locke finished his story before they reached the hotel.

"Jesus," Cooper said. "We're sittin' ducks here."

"Yeah, we are," Locke said. "Whether they were after the payroll or just reputation hunting, we are."

"Maybe we ought to camp outside of town, wait for the train up the tracks some. That clerk can send a message for them to stop and unload the gold there."

"Nah," Locke said. "Out in the middle of nowhere, we'd have less cover than we do here. By the way, let's stop at the sheriff's office."

"What for?" Cooper asked. "You said you weren't in trouble."

"He's out looking for you, too," Locke said. "Thought you might be causing more trouble at the whorehouse."

"Hey, that wasn't my fault!"

"I told him that. Let's just put his mind at ease, huh?"

They changed direction and headed for the lawman's office.

When they entered, they saw Maddox sitting behind his desk, drinking coffee.

"You found him," he said.

"Yeah, at Little Annie's."

"Figured you'd find him," Maddox said, "when I saw he wasn't at Pretty Polly's or at Lucky Lil's."

"Why are all the places here named after women?" Cooper asked.

"Are they?" Maddox replied. "Yeah, I guess they are. I hadn't ever noticed before. What're you boys gonna do now?"

"Turn in," Locke said. "Might be safer just to stay in our room."

"Sounds like a good idea to me," Maddox said. "You might want to set yerself up some kind of warning system, though. Just in case somebody else gets it into their head to come at you."

"That's good advice, Sheriff," Locke said. "We'll take it. Thanks."

"Don't mention it," Maddox said. "Word I get on the train is that it'll be here tomorrow evening. You plannin' on movin' right out?"

"No," Locke said. "We made other arrangements."

He told Maddox about renting the livery for the night and spending the night there with the gold.

"I'll come by from time to time to check on you," Maddox said when Locke was done.

"Fine," Locke said. "We'll move out at first light the next morning."

"You'll be on your own, then."

"Figured we were on our own now," Locke said. "Obliged to you for taking an interest."

"Just tryin' to keep things quiet in my town."

Locke and Cooper both wished the man a good night and left.

When they got to their room, they were removing their boots when Cooper asked, "You ever wonder how the sheriff knew that the payroll shipment was gonna be in gold?"

"Yeah," Locke said. "I wondered that right off."

Cooper looked at Locke over his shoulder. "Think he might be plannin' somethin'?" he asked. "Maybe he sent those two after you."

"Could be," Locke said. "I just figured from the start that we'd suspect everybody."

"That sounds like a good way to figure."

THIRTY-SIX

They set some warning signs around the room—a pitcher on the window sill, a chair in front of the door—and then turned in. The night went by uneventfully, and Locke awoke before Cooper. He just wasn't used to going to bed that early. His eyes popped open even more when the sun started creeping in through the window. He got out of bed without waking Cooper, got dressed, and crept out the door. He decided to see if there was anyplace in town he could get an early breakfast.

In the lobby, he found the same young clerk from the night before and asked him about breakfast.

"Our dining room won't be open for half an hour," the man said, "but there's a place around the corner that would be open now. It's small, but the food's good."

"Thanks, I'll try that. If my friend comes down, would you tell him where I am?"

"Certainly."

Locke nodded and went out the door.

There was a knock on the door of the general store, which wasn't ready to open for another hour yet. Cal Nieves, who opened every morning, went to the door and found Del Morgan there.

"What's goin' on, Del?" Nieves said.

"Did you hear what happened last night?" Morgan asked. "Somebody tried to kill John Locke."

"Where did that happen?"

"Lucky Lil's," Morgan said. "The way I heard it, one of the girls, Katy, was paid to take Locke upstairs, and then two men with guns broke in and tried to kill him."

"What happened?"

"They killed Katy, he killed them. He's the only one who walked away from it."

"Do you think it was about the payroll?"

"I don't know," Morgan said. "It might just be someone who recognized him and wanted to make a name for themselves."

"Any idea who the men were?"

"Strangers."

Nieves and Morgan both leaned against the counter, deep in thought.

"Del, are you thinkin' we should move our timetable up?" Nieves finally asked.

"I don't see how we can," Morgan said. "We can't do nothin' until the payroll actually gets here."

"I can't help thinkin' it would have been good for us if

Locke had been killed," Nieves said. "Then we'd only have that old marshal to deal with."

"Well, it didn't happen, so we'll never know what would have happened if Locke was killed."

"Unless somebody kills him."

Morgan stood up straight. "I ain't no murderer, Cal."

"Del," Nieves said, "this was your idea. Do you really think we're gonna be able to take that payroll from these two men without shots bein' fired? Without somebody getting killed?"

"I thought if they saw they were outnumbered, they'd give it up."

"These men don't have reputations for giving up," Nieves pointed out. "You and me convinced the others to go along with that, Del. We can't just give it up."

"I don't want to give it up."

"Then you better be ready to kill somebody."

"Not in cold blood!" Morgan said. "I ain't about to ambush somebody or back-shoot them."

"But if you have to shoot to kill to get the payroll?"

Morgan hesitated, then said, "If it comes to that, I will."

THIRTY-SEVEN

D ale Cooper appeared at the café around the corner from the hotel while Locke was eating his breakfast.

"Mornin'," he said, sitting across from him. When the waiter came over, he pointed at Locke's plate of steak and eggs. "I'll have the same."

"Comin' up, sir."

"You slept well," Locke said.

"I slept the sleep of the just," Cooper said. "Resisting that whiskey was good for me last night."

"And it helped that no one tried to kill us."

"That's always helpful."

"Any ideas about what we should do today?" Cooper asked.

"Yeah, I had one," Locke said. "I think we should stay together and stay in one place today."

"Like where?"

"The train station."

Cooper shrugged. "That's good for me. We'll sit around, talk, smoke, maybe you'll even think up an answer to the question I asked you."

"What question?"

"The one about what you'd do with all that gold."

Locke put his fork down and sat back. "I told you, I don't think about stuff like that," Locke said. "I'm happy with who I am, Coop. That much money would change me."

"Change," Cooper said, shaking his head. "I sure could use some change about now."

The waiter came and put a plate of steak and eggs in front of him, then withdrew.

"It doesn't do any good to think like that," Locke said. "You want to change your life, deliver this gold, and then go do it."

"Easy for you to say," Cooper replied. "You're young."

"I'm younger than you," Locke said, "but that doesn't make me a young man."

"Oh, yeah? Gimme back ten years—the last ten years—and I'll show you what I'd do with it."

"Do something with the next ten, Coop," Locke said. "That makes more sense."

"Yeah," Cooper said. "Maybe . . ."

They ate the rest of their breakfast in silence, Cooper cleaning his plate like a man who had never had a drinking problem.

"I guess we should check out of the hotel and take our gear to the train station," Cooper said when he was done. "Along with the buckboard."

"Yeah," Locke said." We can go right from there to the livery."

"I was thinkin'," Cooper said. "We got to get on the trail sometime, why not just do it? Stayin' in town one more night, that just gives somebody another chance to try for us— whatever their reason."

Locke thought a moment, then nodded. "You might be right about that—unless the train comes in after dark."

"We can find that out when we get over there."

"All right, let's check out, then get the buckboard and our horses from the livery. We can tell Mr. Milty what we're planning and that we'll pay him something even if we don't use the livery."

"We can also find out if his kid delivered our message."

"Right."

They paid their bill and left the café. As they were aproaching the hotel, they saw young Frank Milty waiting out front.

"Mr. Locke, Mr. Cooper," Frank said as they reached him. "I delivered your note."

"And?" Cooper asked.

"I got one in return."

He took a crumpled piece of paper from his pocket and handed it over. In return, Locke gave him the rest of his money.

"Thanks, Frank," he said. "You did a good job."

"If you need me again, just let me know," the young boy said.

"We'll do that."

The boy nodded and ran off, to do whatever it was boys his age did with their money.

"What's it say?" Locke asked.

"Crowell says Molly is out at the creek already. He's gonna send someone out to tell her what's going on. He says he thinks she'll just stay there and wait for us." He passed the note to Locke. "Says she likes bein' alone."

"Poor George," Locke said, scanning the note. "He's so in love with her it's painful to watch."

"Think she knows?"

Locke folded the note and tucked it into his pocket. "She knows. A woman always knows."

"That sounds like you're speaking from personal experience, John. Some woman break your heart?"

"More than one, my friend," Locke said. "More than one . . ."

Hoke Benson and his men were staying at a hotel on the other side of town, a cheap, rundown place with no name.

"We coulda stayed at a better place," Eli Jordan complained as they met in the lobby. Hoke had his own room, but Eli and Bob Bailey shared one.

"Go ahead," Hoke said.

"You won't let us use any of the first payroll money," Eli complained.

"We don't wanna be flashin' any money, Eli," Hoke said. "After we hit the second payroll, we'll put some distance between us and this place, and you can spend all the money you want."

"I can't wait."

"Where's Bailey?"

"He went over to the station like you tol' him," Eli said. "He should be right here."

Right on cue, Bailey walked through the front door.

"What's goin' on with Locke and Cooper?" Hoke asked.

"It looks like they checked out of their hotel. They got their buckboard and horses from the livery and took everything over to the station with them."

"They're gonna leave right from the train station, soon as they get the payroll."

"How do you know that?" Bailey asked.

"I'm figurin' that, Bob," Hoke said. "I don't know that for sure, but that's the way it looks."

"So, what do we do?" Eli said.

"We gotta be ready to leave at any time," Hoke said. "We'll have to talk to Rome and Turpin."

"We really need those guys?" Eli asked.

"You want to go against Cooper and Locke just the three of us?" Hoke asked.

"No, but do we have to cut them in for an equal share?" Eli complained.

"Actually," Hoke said, "no."

Eddie Rome looked out the window of his hotel. In quality, it was about halfway between the Gold Nugget, where Locke was staying, and the no-name where Hoke Benson was staying. As far as location, it was in the center of town. Rome was able to see Locke and Cooper on their way to the livery, and he saw Bob Bailey walking to the station. He also saw Locke and Cooper taking their buckboard and horses to the station.

When he met his partner, Turpin, in the hotel dining room for breakfast, he said, "Somethin's happenin'."

"Like what?"

"Bacon and eggs," Rome said to the waiter. "Locke and Cooper collected their stuff from the livery and took it to the train station. I think they're gonna leave town as soon as they get the payroll."

"Think Hoke knows?"

"He knows."

"So, what do we do?"

"We wait," Rome said. "Hoke'll send Eli over to tell us what to do."

"Eddie."

"Yeah?" Rome sat back to allow the waiter to put down his plate.

"You're smarter than Hoke, ain'tcha?"

"Sure I am," Rome said.

"Then why are we lettin' him tell us what to do?" Turpin asked.

"Because it was his idea."

"So?"

"So, we let him do all the work and all the plannin', and then we take the money from him and the others."

"And kill 'em?"

"Of course," Rome said. "Why would we leave them alive to come after us?"

"I just wanted to make sure," Turpin said.

THIRTY-EIGHT

Locke and Cooper sat on a wooden bench on the train platform with their backs to a wall.

"This ain't no secret, you know," Sheriff Maddox said. "You drove right through the center of town."

They both turned their heads to look at him.

"We know that," Locke said.

"You just gonna sit here all day?" the lawman asked.

"Until the train arrives."

Maddox looked around. "I can't stay here with you," he said.

"We know that."

Maddox shifted from foot to foot.

"Sheriff," Locke said, "we'll be fine. Go look after your town."

"Just think," Cooper added. "If somethin' happens here, it's outside of town."

"I'll keep that in mind," Maddox said.

"He's not a bad guy," Cooper said as Sheriff Maddox walked off the platform.

"I guess."

"You don't think so?"

"I think he's having problems with us being here," Locke said. "I think he's been real comfortable up to now."

"And we're makin' him uncomfortable?"

"Very."

"Maybe he'll become a real lawman again."

"You don't know his past," Cooper said. "How do you know he didn't put in a lot of years as a real lawman? How do you know he doesn't deserve to take it easy here?"

"I don't know, Coop," Locke said. "Do you?"

"No," Cooper said. "I don't know nothin' about him."

"Why don't we just worry about why we're here, then?" Locke suggested. "Worry about the payroll, and about watching each other's back."

"Okay," Cooper said. "Okay."

Later in the afternoon, the clerk came out and told them the train would arrive within the hour.

"Still early enough for us to put some distance between us and this town," Cooper said.

"Depending on how long it takes us to unload the gold," Locke said. "I've got no idea how big or how heavy the load is, do you?"

Cooper was about to answer when they both heard it, the sound of the train whistle.

"It's early," the clerk said, sticking his head out the door.

"Here comes all that gold," Cooper said, his tone almost reverent.

"What do we have to show that we're pickin' it up?" Locke asked as they both stood up.

"I got a paper from Molly," Cooper said, "and she sent a telegram with my name on it. We won't have any trouble takin' delivery."

Sheriff Maddox appeared at the end of the platform and started walking toward them.

"Looks like somebody else heard the train whistle," Locke said.

"Sheriff Maddox," Cooper said.

"Thought I'd stop by and see if somebody got brave."

"Appreciate the thought, Sheriff," Locke said.

When the train pulled in, Locke, Cooper, and Sheriff Maddox made their way to the payroll car. The door slid open, and two men with rifles appeared. Cooper stepped forward and produced the paper Molly had given them for identification.

"Sheriff?" one of them asked, looking at Maddox.

"What are you askin' him for?" Cooper demanded.

"He's the law, ain't he?"

"I got identification right there," Cooper said. "Signed by Molly Shillstone. What more do you need?"

"How do I know you're Cooper?" the man demanded.

Cooper turned and looked at Locke.

"I'll vouch for him."

The guard looked at Locke. "And who are you?"

"Is my name on that paper?" Locke asked Cooper.

"No."

"I guess I can't help, then."

Cooper sighed, then looked at Maddox. "Sheriff?"

The guard looked at the lawman.

"He's Dale Cooper."

The guard looked at the name on the paper again, then said to his partner, "Okay." He looked at Cooper. "We got four crates of gold."

"Bars?" Cooper asked.

"Coins."

They turned out to be small crates, but heavy. The guards would not leave the car, as they had other valuables there. Locke and Cooper had to carry the crates themselves, one in front, one in back, each with a hand on his gun. A small crowd gathered to watch them.

"Word gets around fast," Locke said.

Maddox, who walked alongside them, said, "I'll stay with the first crate while you get the second."

Then he stayed with the first two while they got the third, and then the fourth. By that time, it seemed as if half the town had turned out to watch them unload.

"They're going to come out of the woodwork for this," Maddox said.

"We have to get moving," Cooper said. "Once we're out of sight, a lot of these people will forget all about it."

"And the others?" Maddox asked.

"They might come after us," Cooper said. "We'll deal with them when they do."

"I don't envy you this job," Maddox said.

Cooper tossed a tarp over the crates, closed the tailgate

of the buckboard, and turned to face Maddox. "You want to come with us?"

"Oh, no," Maddox said. "I'm not getting paid enough to paint that kind of a target on my back."

"No," Locke said. "We are."

As Locke and Cooper rode off with the buckboard full of gold, Hoke Benson pushed through the crowd to watch them go. As the people began to disperse, he remained there. With this many people aware of what was on that buckboard, he knew they were going to have competition. That meant they were going to have to try to hit the payroll on the trail to Turnback Creek.

He waited for Sheriff Maddox to move away with the rest of the crowd, then turned to go back to Lucky Lil's and pick up his men.

"Now?" Eli asked.

"Come on. Get up. We've got to get mounted and ride."

"What's goin' on?" Rome asked, coming over from his table.

"We're movin'!" Hoke said.

"Now?"

"Yes, now!" he shouted. "What's so hard to understand about that?"

He headed for the door, and the other men hurried to keep up with him.

From the back of the crowd, Cal Nieves and Del Morgan watched the gold get loaded into the buckboard.

"Let's go and find the others," Morgan said. "We've got to move now."

"Are you ready for this, Del?" Nieves asked.

"Did you see them loading those crates?" Morgan asked. "That's gold, Cal. Believe me, I'm ready."

When Hoke and his men got to the livery, they saw five men riding away at high speed.

"Hey," Hoke shouted at the liveryman. "We need our horses, fast!"

"You got an emergency?" Ed Milty asked.

"Yeah, mister," Hoke said. "We got a big emergency."

"That's funny," Milty said. "That's what those five who just rode out of here said. Wonder what kind of emergency they had?"

"I think I know," Hoke said. "Come on, we'll help you get those horses."

Locke looked at Cooper, who was looking behind them. "Coop?"

"You saw that crowd," the ex-marshal said. "Somebody's got to try us early."

"That's okay," Locke said, touching the rifle next to him. "We'll be ready."

THIRTY-NINE

They managed to put some distance between themselves and Kingdom Junction, even though the weight
of the gold slowed them down, and then they stopped.

Locke dropped down from the buckboard. "We might
as well wait for them."

"How many do you think will come?" Cooper asked.

"However many they can gather while they're in heat
for the gold," Locke said. "I don't expect this to be a very
organized attempt."

"Not the ones who hit the first payroll yet."

"No," Locke said. "You saw the looks on the faces of
those people. Some of them were salivating. Believe me,
somebody's going to be coming along, and soon."

"Well," Cooper said, "we can't outrun them, that's for
sure. Guess you're right. We might as well wait."

They had stopped near a clump of trees and a formation of rocks.

"I'll take the rocks," Locke said, "and you take the trees. We'll have them in a crossfire."

"How close do we let them get to the gold?"

"All the way," Locke said.

The first group of five riders came within sight of the buckboard and stopped.

"This was a bad idea," Malcolm Turner said. "We ain't robbers."

"Don't get cold feet on us, Malcolm," Del Morgan said. "Do you know how much gold is on that buckboard?"

"I don't," Cal Nieves said.

"Anybody know?"

The other men all exchanged looks and shrugs.

"Well," Morgan said, "we know it's a lot. Four boxes worth. And it's just sittin' there."

"Yeah," Cletus Cloninger said, "but why is it just sittin' there?"

"That's easy," Malcolm said. "They got scared. They ran off." His tone was hopeful.

"I think we should go down and find out," Cal said, drawing his gun. "Are you with me?"

"Now, hold on, Cal," Morgan said. "You were the one who was tellin' me what kind of men we're dealin' with. The kind that don't give up."

"Well," Nieves said, "maybe I was wrong. Maybe they did give up. Maybe they just ran off."

Morgan looked into Nieves's feverish eyes and knew what he was seeing: gold fever.

"Are you with me?" he asked again.

The other three men nodded and drew their guns. Morgan knew he couldn't have stopped them if he tried.

"Hold it!" Hoke said, holding up his hand.

The four riders behind him reined their horses in.

"They got here first," Eli said, watching the five riders approach the buckboard. "They had the same idea we had, five against two. They're gonna get our gold."

"They're not gonna get anything," Hoke said.

"Come on," Turpin said. "We can ride there and take it from them after they take it from the other two."

"Where are the other two?" Bailey asked.

"They're there," Hoke said. "They didn't just ride off and leave all that gold."

"You think so?" Eli asked.

"I know so."

"So, let's just set here and watch and see what happens," Rome suggested.

"That's a very good idea," Hoke said, dismounting. The other men followed, and he told Bailey, "Take the horses back about a hundred yards and keep 'em quiet."

"I don't get to watch?" he complained.

"That's right, Bob," Hoke said. "You don't get to watch. Do like I told you."

Muttering, Bailey collected the reins of everyone's horses and started walking.

"We're just gonna watch," Hoke said, crouching down. "Has everyone got that?"

They all got it, and crouched down.

* * *

Cal Nieves led his four companions right up to the gold-laden buckboard, with Del Morgan bringing up the rear. The whole thing had been his idea, but he knew he had lost control of the situation. Even Red Sinclair's normally stoic face was showing gold fever.

"Whaddaya think, Cal?" Malcolm asked. "Are they gone?"

All five men started looking around them with puzzled but hungry faces.

"Wait a minute," Cloninger asked. "What if they switched buckboards on us?"

"Yeah," Malcolm said. "What if there ain't no gold under that tarp?"

"Del?" Cal asked.

"Well," Del said, "check it, Cal."

"Me?"

"Yeah," Del said. "Look under the tarp."

Cal dismounted, climbed into the back of the buckboard, and lifted the tarp. "Looks like the crates are here," he said.

They waited again for someone to come forward, but nobody did.

"Open one up, Cal," Malcolm shouted. "Come on, open one!"

Nieves took out his knife, which up to now had been used only for cutting twine in the store, jabbed it beneath the top of one crate, and lifted the lid. When he got it off and the sun hit the coins, it was blinding.

"Jesus," he said, taking up a handful of coins. "They're gold coins." He held his hand out for the others to see.

"Well," Cloninger said, dismounting as well, "I guess it's ours. We're rich, boys!"

Whooping and hollering, the other men dismounted and started for the buckboard. That's when Locke and Cooper stepped into view, their rifles in their hands.

"Not today, boys!" Cooper shouted, firing his rifle once to get their attention. "It's a bad day to get rich—or dead."

FORTY

All five men froze, two of them staring at Dale Cooper, the other three at John Locke. Cooper looked at the handful of gold Cal Nieves had.

"You got a lot of money in gold in your hand, son," Cooper said to him. "What do you want to do about it?"

Cal stared into Cooper's eyes. His left hand was filled with gold, so his right hand was free to go for his gun if he wanted to. "Del?" he said.

Locke noticed one of the men move his head and figured this was Del, the leader. "Don't make any mistakes, boy," he said.

Del looked over at Locke. His mistake had already been made. He'd let them all ride down to the buckboard, and now they were faced with their moment of truth. Five against two for all the gold on the buckboard.

"There's a lot of gold here," Del said to Locke and Cooper. "Plenty for all of us."

The looks in all of their eyes were unmistakable to Locke. They were going to make a mistake that they would all have to pay for.

"Don't do it, boy," Cooper said, reading Del's body language from behind.

"Shit—" Cal said.

Cal went for his gun, too impatient for Del to call the play. Also, the weight of the gold in his left hand convinced him it was worth it.

Locke moved the muzzle of his rifle a fraction of an inch and shot him dead. Cal was thrown from the buckboard, the gold in his left hand flying through the air like a shower of gold. Clete Cloninger went for his own weapon. Cooper fired once. The bullet hit Cloninger in the chest and drove him to the ground, where he lay still.

"Don't—" Malcolm Turner said, but Cooper fired again and took him from his saddle.

That left Del Morgan and Red Sinclair, both of whom were scrambling for their weapons. Morgan, never a hand with a gun, had his go flying from his grip even before Cooper's bullet struck him. Sinclair was such a huge target that both Locke and Cooper put bullets in him. The big man sat on his saddle for a few moments, looking puzzled, before he slumped and fell to the ground.

Locke walked over to the bodies, checked them, then turned to look at Cooper. "They're all dead."

"Their choice," the ex-marshal said, thumbing fresh rounds into his rifle. "These two," he said, pointing to the last two he and Cooper had gunned down, "might have given up, given another choice."

"We couldn't take the chance."

Locke looked around. Three shots from Cooper's rifle, three kills. The older man was sure shooting better than he had in town. Looking at him now, there was no sign of the shakes.

Locke reloaded his own rifle, then walked to his horse and slid the rifle into its scabbard.

"We'll have to bury them," he said.

"Why?" Cooper asked. "There could be more comin'."

"There probably are," Locke said, "but we just can't leave them out here."

"We don't have a shovel," Cooper said. "How are we gonna dig five graves?"

Locke was stuck for an answer.

"And we can't turn around and take them back to town," Cooper went on. "We got a job to do."

Locke looked down at the five dead men. He was willing to bet at least two of them had never stolen anything in their lives. The lure of the gold had brought them out there to die.

"We can cover their bodies with rocks," he said. "That's the least we can do."

"Fine," Cooper said. "We'll put them all together and do it, and then we can get out of here. Somebody might come along and find them." He put his rifle on the front seat of the buckboard. "Come on," he said. "We'll carry them behind them rocks you were hidin' behind."

"They put their rifles down," Turpin said. "Why don't we go down and take the gold now?"

"Shut up, Roy," Rome said.

"You see that?" Eli asked. "They gunned them just as easy as you please."

"I saw," Hoke said. "Come on, let's get to the horses."

"We gonna take 'em?" Turpin asked.

"No," Hoke said before Rome could tell the man to shut up again. "We're gonna get more men."

Locke and Cooper dumped the men behind the rocks and then covered them with as many stones as they could find and stack. They were sweating heavily by the time they were done, despite the fact that it was cool. Clouds were rolling in, and it would be raining probably within the hour.

They donned their slickers in anticipation of the rain, then Locke mounted his horse, and Cooper climbed aboard the buckboard.

"You sayin' I overreacted?" Cooper asked before they started.

"I'm not saying that."

"Then what are you sayin'?"

"Just that they might've given up," Locke said, "given the chance. That's all."

"And then they would have gone and got more men and came back for the gold."

"You might be right."

Cooper looked at the sky. "Let's see how many miles we can cover before the sky opens up."

FORTY-ONE

They continued on despite the rain, as it came down in a sort of mist rather than a downpour. But eventually they had to stop because of darkness. When they made camp, the rain had let up, so they were able to build a fire and make some coffee. They made a meal of dry beef jerky and canned peaches.

"I'm sorry if you don't agree with what we did back there," Cooper said from across the fire.

"Forget it," Locke said. "It's the first action you've seen like that in a while, isn't it?"

"Yeah," Cooper said. "First in a while." They sat in silence for a moment. "I did okay, though, didn't I?"

"You did better than okay, Coop," Locke said. "You were as steady as a rock."

"Was I?" Cooper asked. "Not inside. I could use a drink."

"We didn't bring any whiskey."

Cooper looked away.

"Coop, did you bring a bottle?"

Cooper hesitated, then said, "In my saddlebag."

Locke thought about getting the bottle and smashing it, then decided not to. Might be better for Cooper to be resisting it. "Have a cigarette instead."

"Think I will."

Locke watched the man roll a cigarette with steady hands, then light it with a twig from the fire.

"I'll take the first watch," Locke offered.

"I'll turn in after this cigarette."

Locke had another cup of coffee, noticed that Cooper was staring into the fire, breaking a cardinal rule. If anyone had hit them at that moment, Cooper would have had no night vision for several minutes—long enough to get them both killed. He'd have to remind the man when he woke him not to look into the fire.

Cooper flicked the remainder of his cigarette into the fire and got to his feet with a groan. "Wake me whenever you like," he said. "I haven't stood watch in a long time, either. I'm lookin' forward to it."

"It has been a long time, hasn't it?" Locke said.

Cooper rolled himself up in his bedroll underneath the buckboard in case it rained again. He was keeping his slicker between himself and the wet ground in the hopes of staying dry while he slept.

Locke turned to the fire and prepared another pot of coffee.

Hoke Benson and his men were back in Kingdom Junction when it started to rain.

"Rome, you come with me," Hoke said. "The rest of you, get to your hotel rooms. We'll be leaving at first light."

"We're letting them get ahead of us," Eli said.

"We know where they're goin', Eli," Hoke said. "It's no secret, after all."

"What about a drink?" Turpin said.

"Hotel," Rome said. "No drinkin' tonight, Roy."

"Right."

Hoke gave the reins of his horse to Bailey, as did Rome, and the two men walked away together.

Hoke and Rome went to Lucky Lil's and got a beer each.

"They worked well together," Rome said. "That ain't good news."

"They're supposed to be past it," Hoke said. "The old man's a drunk."

"He didn't look like a drunk to me," Rome said.

"No, he didn't. That's why we need more men. Do you know anyone who'd be interested?"

"Plenty of 'em, once they hear about the gold."

"What if they don't hear about the gold?"

Rome swallowed some beer and asked, "Whaddaya mean?"

"What if we just hire a few more guns?"

"And not cut them in for equal shares?"

"Right."

"And how do we keep them from knowing about the gold?" Rome asked.

Hoke stared at Rome. "We don't tell them."

"What if they want to know what Locke and Cooper are delivering?" the other man asked.

"They're just being hired for a job, that's it," Hoke said. "We'll pay them well, but they're hired help."

"Like me?"

"You're gettin' an equal share, Rome," Hoke said.

"All right," Rome said. "I'll get . . . two more men?"

"Yeah, two," Hoke said. "We need them tonight. Have them meet us at the livery at first light."

"Okay," Rome said. He looked around the room. "I see a couple here I can ask."

"I'm turnin' in," Hoke said. "You see who you can recruit and I'll see you in the mornin'."

"Right."

Hoke left the saloon, and Rome went to get another beer.

FORTY-TWO

Locke and Cooper got an early start the next morning. When Locke had awakened Cooper for his turn on watch he made himself tell his friend about looking into the fire . . .

"I know that, John," Cooper said, irritably. "I haven't completely lost my mind."

"It's just that . . . earlier last night you were—"

"I was what?"

"Looking into the fire."

"Was I?" Cooper paused to think. "Well, all right. I'll be sure not to while I'm on watch. Satisfied?"

"Okay," Locke said. "Okay."

When Cooper woke Locke in the morning he handed him a fresh cup of coffee.

"Sorry I snapped at you this morning," he said. "You're

right, I was lookin' into the fire. Won't happen again."

"Thanks for the coffee . . ."

Hoke arrived at the livery and found six men waiting for him there. Eli nervously pulled him aside.

"Who are these other two?" he asked.

"Just hired guns, Eli."

"They gettin' an equal share?"

"No," Hoke said, "and shut up about it."

They returned to the other men, and Rome said, "Hoke, this is Joe Bently and Stan Sharp."

Two men, tall and lean, in their forties. To Hoke Benson, they were just extra guns. He forgot their names moments later.

"Fine," Hoke said. "Let's just mount up and get going. We're probably going to have to take them on the mountain now."

"They're hauling a heavy load," Eli said. "Why not catch up to them and take them before then?"

"They'll reach the mountain before we can reach them," Hoke said. "There's no point in pushing the horses."

"What's so heavy about a mining payroll?" Sharp wanted to know.

Hoke gave Eli a hard look and said, "Nothing. Forget it. Let's just get mounted and move out."

Locke and Cooper made good time and were only two hours late—plus two days—meeting Molly Shillstone by Turnback Creek, where she was camped. She was wearing men's clothes—shirt, jeans, boots, and a hat—but she looked very elegant nonetheless.

"How about some coffee?" she asked as they dismounted.

"Sorry we're late," Cooper said. "We got hit on the trail, and the rain slowed us down."

"Wait, wait," Molly said, handing them each a cup of coffee. "Somebody tried for my gold already?"

Cooper told her the story of the five men on the road, then added the two in Kingdom Junction who tried for Locke.

"And you killed them all?"

"Yes."

"I'm impressed," she said. "Good job." She looked at Locke. "I guess I hired the right men for the job, after all."

"I guess so," Locke said.

"Will you be camping here overnight?" she asked.

"That's up to Marshal Cooper," Locke told her. "He's still in charge of this job."

"We've still got an hour or two of daylight," Cooper started. "We really should keep—"

"I'm staying here tonight and heading back in the morning," Molly said, interrupting. "I really could use the company. I've been here for two days alone. I like being alone, but now I'm done with it."

Cooper looked over at Locke, who simply shrugged. "Well, all right," Cooper said, "but you have to do the cooking."

Molly smiled, looked over at Locke, and said, "Agreed."

She prepared bacon and beans, which was a feast com-

pared with the jerky they'd been eating. They sat around
the fire as it started to get dark and ate. Behind them, they
could hear the creek running.

Molly wanted to hear more about the men who tried
to steal the gold, and Locke left it to Cooper to tell her—
and he did so, with a flourish. He made the gun battle
sound much more dangerous than it was. In truth, he and
Locke had so outclassed the four men that they didn't
have a chance. It sounded to Locke as if his old friend had
enjoyed gunning them down.

When Cooper turned in—out in the open, because the
rain seemed to have let up for a while—Molly poured Locke
another cup of coffee and sat across the fire from him.

"Marshal Cooper sounds as if the events of yesterday
excited him," she said.

"I'm afraid they did."

"You didn't find it exciting?"

He looked across the fire at her. "I don't find anything
particularly exciting about killing men, Mrs. Shillstone,"
he replied.

"Never?" she asked. "You never have?"

"No."

"A man of your reputation?"

"What do you know about my reputation?" he asked.

"Well . . . only what I've heard."

"That I'm a cold-blooded killer?" he asked. "Have you
ever heard that about me?"

"Well . . ."

"Maybe you have," he said, not waiting for her to find
an answer. "Maybe that's been said about me, but a repu-

tation is not a man, Molly. It hardly ever describes a man at all, not truly."

After a moment, she said, "I'm sorry. I was just trying to make conversation. I was stupid—"

"Never mind," Locke said. "It doesn't matter. At this point in my life, it doesn't make much difference. I've had to play the cards I was dealt for so many years . . ."

"Why do men do that?"

"What?"

"Use gambling terms to describe their lives?"

"Do we?"

"Yes, you do," she said. "All of you. My father did it all the time, and he wasn't even a gambler."

"Wasn't he?" he asked. "Aren't you?"

"Maybe," she said. "Maybe he was, and maybe I am, but if so, then we only ever bet on sure things."

"Ah," Locke said, "but the first thing you learn as a gambler is that there's no such thing as a sure thing."

"Mines," she said.

"What?"

She stood up and looked toward the mountain. "My father knew from a look, a smell, that a mine was a sure thing," she said, "and he taught me how to do it." She pointed. "This mine was a sure thing from the beginning, and it still is."

"As long as you can pay your men," Locke said.

"That's right."

"And if you can't?"

She turned and came back to the fire, hunkered down by it, and looked across at him. "I'll lose it."

"Why?"

"I have notes to pay," she said. "If I can't pay them, the bank will take the mine."

"Who knows that?"

She shrugged. "Me, George, the bank . . . and now you."

"No one else?"

"No one else should," she said. "Why are you asking?"

"Just making conversation."

"You think someone is stealing my payroll to make me miss my loan payments?"

"I don't know, Molly," he said. "It's a possibility, I guess."

She sat back on her haunches and gave it some thought.

"I never considered . . ." she said with wonder. "I thought it was just robbers after the money, and now the gold. But maybe what you're saying makes sense . . ."

"I don't know if it does or doesn't, Molly," Locke replied. "Like I said, I was just talking."

"No, no," she said. "You're making sense—this makes sense." She got to her feet, started to pace. "This makes perfect sense. Son of a bitch! Why didn't I see this before?"

"Molly," Locke said, standing up, "calm down. This is your business, not mine. I don't know what the hell I'm talking about."

"But maybe you do, don't you see?" she asked.

He took hold of her shoulders to stop her from pacing. "I'm just saying, don't go off half cocked," he told her. "Think about this awhile before you do anything too foolish."

"Foolish?" she asked. "What makes you think I'm going to do anything foolish?"

"The look on your face," he said. "I've seen it before, mostly on men—and mostly just before they went and did something that got them killed."

She stared at him for a few moments, then nodded and said, "Yes, all right, you're right. I can see that." He dropped his hands, and she stepped back, out of his reach. "I'll give it some more thought. I'm, uh, going to turn in now."

"I'm standing first watch," he said. "I'll wake Coop in four hours."

"What about me?" she asked. "I can stand watch."

"No," he said. "This is what we do. You just get some sleep."

"All right," she said. "All right."

He could see that her mind was still whirling and doubted that she would get right to sleep. He was shocked that something he'd said idly—with no information or knowledge at all to back it up—would have caused such a reaction in her.

But now that the thought was planted, he wondered who she was thinking might be behind something like that? According to her, it could only have been someone from the bank or George Crowell. Loyal George, who worked with her father for so long, and now with her, but who was also in love with her and wasn't getting any of that love back.

Locke wondered what the morning would bring. What would Molly decide to do about this? Maybe he could persuade her not to do anything until he got back. The least he could do after putting the thought in her head was to back whatever play she wanted to make. Also, they needed her alive to pay them the rest of their money when they got back, as she had only paid them half up front.

That's what he'd tell her when she woke up—that it would be bad business to get killed before they came back.

FORTY-THREE

The rain held off all night so that the only wetness John Locke woke up to was the sound of the creek and the cup of hot coffee Molly was holding out to him.

"Thanks."

"Breakfast is ready, and the marshal has already started eating," she told him.

"Okay," Locke said, hauling himself to his feet.

They both walked to the fire, and Locke saw Cooper working on a plate of scrambled eggs.

"Couldn't wait for you," Cooper said. "I'm starved."

"That's fine," Locke said, looking around. He wondered if anyone had caught up to them, might be watching them right now while they ate their breakfast.

"Here you go," Molly said, handing him a plate of eggs.

"Thanks."

She made a plate for herself and sat down across from them.

"How are you feeling this morning?" Locke asked her.

"Better," she said. "Not as angry."

"That's good."

"Angry about what?" Cooper asked.

Locke and Molly looked at each other.

"I'll explain it to you once we get started," Locke said. "It'll give us something to talk about."

Cooper shrugged and went back to his breakfast.

"So, you're not planning to, um, do anything foolish?" Locke asked.

"I never intended to do anything foolish," she said. "I'm just going to do some investigating to see what I can find out."

"Just don't confront anybody until we get back."

"Why?"

"Because," he said slowly, "I don't want anything to happen to you before we get back."

"You're worried about me?" she asked. "That's sweet."

"We're going to need you alive and well to pay us the rest of our money when the job is done."

"Oh, I see," she said. "So, it's not that you're worried about me, specifically."

"It's just good business."

"I see," she said again. "I understand."

"Since you are the good businesswoman that you are," he said, "I knew that you would."

Cooper, if he was listening while he was eating, didn't let his interest show.

They finished the remainder of the coffee and eggs, and then Locke saddled Molly Shillstone's horse for her before saddling his own. While he did that, Cooper was saddling his horse and hitching up the team to the buckboard.

Locke offered to give Molly a leg up onto her horse, which she refused, and she mounted very expertly.

Looking up at her, he asked, "How did you get those eggs out here in one piece?"

"Very carefully," she said.

"Well," he warned her, "be just that careful with everything else until we get back."

"Don't worry," she said. "I'll make sure your money is waiting for you when you get back."

Before he could say anything else, she gigged her horse and rode out of camp at a gallop, toward the town of Turnback Creek.

As they pulled out of camp, with Cooper mounted and Locke driving the buckboard, Cooper said, "So, what was all that stuff about her bein' angry? We do something to get her mad?"

Locke told Cooper about the conversation he'd had with Molly the night before.

"Why'd you go and say a thing like that for and put it in her head?" Cooper asked.

"Like I told her, I was just making conversation," Locke said. "I didn't expect her to react like that."

"You know there doesn't have to be any other motive for somebody to steal a payroll—or gold—than greed."

"I know that."

Cooper paused, stood in his stirrups without stopping, and looked around them.

"What is it?"

"I got that target-on-my-back feeling," Cooper said.

"I've had that since Kingdom Junction," Locke said. "Hell, I've had it all my life."

"I know," Cooper said. "Me, too, but then there comes the time when it really itches, you know?" He sat back down in his saddle. "It sort of makes you feel alive, don't it?"

"I don't need to be shot at to feel alive, Coop," Locke said. "That was quite a story you told Molly last night, by the way."

"I just wanted her to think we were earning our money," Cooper said with a laugh.

"Oh, I think before this is all over, we're going to earn our money," Locke said, "and more."

"I've been thinkin' the same thing," Cooper said.

"About what?"

"That we deserve more money."

"That's not what I said."

"It's just somethin' to think about, John," Cooper replied, "that's all."

FORTY-FOUR

They had a map of routes up to the mine, given to Cooper by Molly Shillstone. According to Molly, if one route was blocked, another should be open. If all established routes were blocked, they would have to find a way to clear one or find a new one themselves.

So far, the first route seemed pretty clear. It was rocky enough so that Locke was glad they were transporting gold and not nitroglycerine, but it was passable.

"According to Molly," Cooper said as they traveled, "this should be the most passable of all."

"Well," Locke said, "so far, so good."

They were both looking around, staying alert, because that target-on-the-back feeling was worse.

"John . . ." Cooper said.

"I feel it."

"You know," Cooper said, "there's a way we can work it so we never have this feeling again."

"I thought you said it made you feel alive."

"It does," Cooper said, "but I also want to stay that way."

"I don't know what you're talking about, Coop," Locke said. He thought he did, but he didn't like what he was thinking.

That's when the first shot came, and then he didn't have time to think anymore, just to react. He launched himself off the buckboard just before the bullet struck the seat where he had been sitting. Cooper also dismounted quickly to take cover.

One shot, and then it was quiet. Cooper's horse galloped off, spooked by the echoing shot. The team was spooked, too, but pulling the heavy gold, they moved only a few yards away and stopped, with Locke's mount tied to the back. This put both of their rifles out of their reach, and they had palmed their six-guns.

"That came from above us," Cooper said. "I saw the bullet hit the buckboard."

"Whoever this is," Locke said, "they knew the route we were going to take and got here ahead of us."

"Somebody who works for Molly," Cooper said. "Not connected with the other five we killed already."

"Agreed."

"Could be one man with a rifle," Cooper said. "Maybe he's just tryin' to get lucky."

"Well, there's one way to find out."

"What are you gonna do?"

"I've got to get to the buckboard before the horses move off any farther," Locke said. "We're going to need a rifle to return fire."

"They're not gonna go far, pullin' that weight."

"Maybe not," Locke said, "but if they drag that buckboard over some rocks and we lose a wheel, we're stuck."

"Good point."

"Watch for his muzzle flash, and cover me," Locke said.

"He's too far away for this," Cooper said, gesturing with his gun, "but at least I can make some noise."

"That's all I can ask."

Locke holstered his own gun, got up into a crouch, and said, "Okay . . . now!"

He took off at a run and sprinted to the buckboard. Three shots were fired from somewhere, and they pinged off the rocks and ground around him. He heard Cooper firing uselessly, but a person's first instinct when he hears shots is to duck, and he was depending on that to make the shooter miss. He hoped he would have accomplished his goal before the shooter realized he was in no danger.

When he reached the buckboard, he quickly hobbled the team so they wouldn't run off. In addition, he placed some stones in front of a couple of the wheels. That done, he made his way to his horse and retrieved his rifle from his saddle. He considered freeing the animal so it could get out of harm's way but was afraid it would run off too far to recover, so he left it tied to the back of the buckboard.

He then signaled to Cooper that he was coming back. This time, the shooter got off more rounds. He probably realized that Cooper was just firing to make noise. One round tugged at Locke's shirt, but he was able to return to Cooper unscathed.

"Where is he?" Locke asked when he reached Cooper.

"Up on that ridge," Cooper said, pointing. "Not ahead of so much as abreast of us."

"Maybe he's just an opportunist who has no idea what we're carrying," Locke said. "Maybe he was just waiting for anyone to come by so he could rob them."

"Whatever he is, he's got us pinned down," Cooper said. "One of us is gonna have to climb up there and get behind him—or at least get close enough to get off a shot."

"One of us?" Locke asked.

"Well," Cooper said, "you looked pretty damned spry running back and forth from the buckboard, and don't forget, you are younger than me by about ten years."

"Eight," Locke said. "It's only eight."

"That still makes my point."

"Don't forget I've got this," Locke said, hefting his rifle. "He doesn't seem to be that good a shot. I could cover you while you grab the buckboard and drive off."

"As bad a shot as he is," Cooper said, "he could still hit one of the horses while he's tryin' to get me."

"Not if I pin him down," Locke said. "All you have to do is get far enough away, and then I can catch up to you on foot."

"He's got to have a horse," Cooper said. "He'll come after you."

"Not if I go after him first," Locke said. "Once we're out of range, I'll mount up and try to find him. You keep going."

Cooper looked at Locke. "If you could just pick him off right from here, our problem would be solved."

"Wouldn't it? I'm a lot better with a handgun than I am with a long one," Locke said. "What about you?"

"The same."

"Well," Locke said, "at least I can keep him busy while you grab the buckboard, and who knows, I might get lucky. After that, I'll try to get closer to him."

"That means I've got to run for the buckboard, huh?"

"That's right," Locke said. "And don't forget, I hobbled the horses, and I blocked a couple of the wheels."

"And wasn't that a real good idea?" Cooper said sarcastically. He was going to have to pause to unhobble the horses and free the wheels.

Locke shrugged. "It seemed one at the time."

FORTY-FIVE

Locke needed the man to fire one more time so he could see where he was for himself.

"I'll spot him as soon as he fires," he told Cooper. "You just keep going."

"If you don't pin him down fast," Cooper said, "I'm as good as a dead man."

"Don't worry," Locke said. "I'll pin him down."

"Okay," Cooper said, indicating he was ready.

"Go."

Cooper started running. The first shot missed him by so much it didn't even ricochet anywhere near them. Locke fired two shots at the ridge, giving Cooper time to get to the buckboard. The first thing the ex-marshal did was to untie Locke's horse and slap it on the rump so that it took off.

"What the—" Locke said.

Cooper kicked away the rocks Locke had put in front of

the wheels, freed the horses, and climbed onto the rear of the buckboard. On a hunch, Locke stopped firing. The man on the ridge didn't fire immediately, and then, when he did shoot at Cooper and the retreating buckboard, the shots went way wild.

Nobody was that bad a shot.

Locke stood up and watched Cooper ride off in the buckboard. The shooter didn't take one shot at him.

"Coop," he said softly, "you son of a bitch."

The shooter was gone, Cooper was gone, and Locke was on foot. His horse had run off, but how far off he didn't know. He just started walking in the direction his horse had gone and in which Cooper had driven the buckboard.

The more he thought about it, the more convinced he became that the shots had been too wild to be honest misses. He hated thinking that the man on the ridge had been working with Cooper, but why else would Cooper have shooed off Locke's horse if not to keep him from following?

Locke remembered the question Cooper had asked him while they were in Kingdom Junction waiting for the train to arrive—asked him more than once, as a matter of fact.

"What would you do with this much gold?"

"What?"

"The gold. If you had it all, what would you do with it?"

"Why are you asking me that?"

"I'm just making conversation . . ."

But he hadn't just been making conversation, had he? He'd been feeling Locke out. Trying to see how Locke would feel about stealing all that gold.

Locke hoped he was wrong. He hoped Cooper had just released his horse to keep it from harm and that the shooter on the ridge had simply been a horrible marksman.

He hoped that his old friend had not been planning to steal the gold right from the beginning.

Right from the goddamn beginning!

Hoke Benson heard the shots and raised his hand for the men to stop. He cocked his head, listening intently. "Hear that?"

"I heard it," Rome said.

"Heard what?" Turpin asked.

"Shut up and listen," Rome said.

They all listened and were eventually rewarded with the sound of more shots.

"Which way?" Hoke asked frantically. "Which way?"

"Ahead," Rome said. "Right ahead of us."

"No," Eli said. "That way—"

"Shut up," Hoke said. "Lead the way, Rome."

FORTY-SIX

It started to rain.

What else could go wrong? Locke was on foot, and his slicker was rolled up on his saddle. Much of this ground was rock and stone, slippery when wet. He'd be lucky not to break an ankle. He was not as surefooted as a horse, or a mule, would have been.

The sky was black. It had been threatening to storm ever since his arrival in Turnback Creek, and now it looked as if the clouds were collecting, swollen almost to bursting with a full-fledged downpour. He had no idea what this mountain would be like in that kind of a rain.

He trudged along, still hoping against hope that he was wrong. He hoped he was overreacting the way he thought Molly had. On the other hand, there was a possibility that if someone were working at cross purposes with Molly, they were working at like purposes with Cooper. Or was he just seeing conspiracy at every turn?

He found himself wondering if Cooper's battle with whiskey were even real. If he was pretending, it would certainly explain his miraculous recovery. Maybe his impaired marksmanship also had been an act. If it all had been faked, then Locke had been taken in because of his friendship. Rather than feeling a fool, he felt betrayed.

But if he had done all that planning, why would he bring Locke into it—a friend, yes, but a friend he hadn't seen in more than ten years? Perhaps even their long friendship was going to be a casualty of one man's desire for gold—a casualty Cooper was willing to risk.

If Cooper actually had played Locke that way, it was something Locke was going to find very hard to forgive.

He certainly wouldn't forget it.

And he definitely would avenge it.

Eddie Rome was the man in the group who could read sign, even on a mountain.

"See the ground? It's been chewed up a bit. The shots were fired here, from above." He rose from his crouch and looked around. "Probably from that ridge."

"Anybody hit?" Hoke asked.

"I don't see any blood," Rome said, "but there were some horses here—at least four."

"Two saddle mounts and a team," Hoke said. "It was them."

"But who was shooting at them?" Rome asked. He looked at Hoke. The other men were too far off to hear them. "Did you send anyone ahead of us? Did you hire somebody yourself?"

"No, of course I didn't," Hoke snapped. "Why would you think that?"

"Maybe you want to cut the rest of us out."

"If I wanted you out, Rome," Hoke said, "I never would have brought you in."

Rome studied Hoke for a few moments, then said, "All right."

"What else can you tell?"

"Not much," Rome said. "Whatever happened, it doesn't appear that anyone was hurt, and they seem to have moved on."

"So, that's what we'll do," Hoke said. "We'll keep moving on."

That's when it started to rain.

Locke couldn't believe his eyes. The horse ahead of him was not his, it was Cooper's. It apparently had stopped to drink some water from a puddle. He approached the animal slowly, but it was so intent on drinking that it ignored him. He was able to grab the reins and take control of the animal. Once the horse had drunk its fill, he led it away from the puddle and started going through the saddlebags. There was nothing there that indicated that Cooper had been planning to steal the gold. Cooper's slicker was rolled up on the saddle, though, so Locke removed it and donned it. He closed the saddlebags and mounted up. Cooper's rifle was still in its scabbard, so Locke had to hold his. He cradled it in the crook of one arm, covering it with the slicker, and controlled the horse with the other hand. At least when he caught up to Cooper, he'd have him completely out-gunned.

"Let's go, boy," he said, and started the animal forward.

On horseback, he should have been able to catch up to the buckboard fairly quickly. However, he was still at a distinct disadvantage. If Cooper were stealing the gold, he would not stay on this route, which led to the mine. He'd choose another, one that would lead him off the mountain. The question was, would he double back off the mountain or keep going over and down the other side? If he doubled back, he might run into someone else who was planning to steal the gold. That first group of five could not be the only ones. So, he'd keep heading up. He had a map from Molly with alternative routes—or did he?

Locke reined the horse in and went through the saddlebags again. Sure enough, he found the map Molly had given to Cooper. The only thing was, all the alternative routes ultimately led to the mine. Cooper needed a route that would lead him away from the mine and over the mountain. If he had planned this, then he would have planned a route as well. The man Locke had known all those years ago was that thorough.

Locke could assume his friend was stealing the gold and try to find that other route, or he could head for the mine and hope he was wrong and that Cooper would be there ahead of him, waiting.

No, even to think that at this point was to make a fool of himself—and he didn't need to do that, because Cooper had done a fine enough job of it, already.

* * *

"How do we know which way they're goin'?" Eli asked aloud, to be heard above the sound of the rain.

"There are three routes to the mine, remember?" Hoke asked. "We found that out early on. Besides, Rome can track them."

"Even over a mountain?" Eli asked. "In the rain?"

"He can track a grain of sand through the desert," Hoke said. "That's why I recruited him."

"But what if—"

He was talking to the wind, though, because Hoke had gigged his horse and was riding ahead to catch up to Rome, who was riding point. Eli didn't like how much time Hoke was spending with Rome. He was starting to wonder who was going to cut whom out when the time came.

"Do you know where we're goin'?" he asked.

"There's something wrong."

"What?"

Rome looked at Hoke. "They ain't together anymore."

"What? They split up?" Hoke demanded. "Why would they do that? Who's got the gold?"

"That's easy," Rome said. "The one with the buckboard has the gold, but—"

"But what?"

"It looks to me like one man's trailin' behind the buck-board, and the fourth horse . . . well, I've lost the fourth horse. It could be anywhere."

"How could you lose it?"

"It's not on this trail," Rome said. "My guess is, it got loose when the shootin' started back there."

"Okay," Hoke said. "Okay, we don't have to be worried about a loose horse."

Rome looked around and said, "We might have to worry about whoever was doin' the shootin'. Might be competition for us."

"We got enough men to take care of any competition," Hoke assured him. "You just keep trackin'."

"As long as I can," Rome said.

"What does that mean?"

"Just what I said," the man answered. "It keeps rainin' like this, it's gonna be hard to read sign."

"Just do the best you can," Hoke said.

"I'm doin' just that already, Hoke," Rome said, gritting his teeth. "I'm doin' just that."

FORTY-SEVEN

Locke had been hoping to catch up to Cooper before nightfall, but that obviously was not going to happen. He found an overhanging rock formation to camp under, with enough room for him and the horse. It kept them fairly dry, and his slicker did the rest for him. He had some beef jerky that night and, in the morning, cleaned his weapons to make sure they were dry and in working order and started out again.

Locke had never been a great sign reader, and the rain was washing away any hope he had of following a trail. He could be wandering this whole mountain for days while Cooper made it to the other side and got far, far away. He was starting to think his best bet was to go to the mine.

That was before he found the body.

The sun was trying to poke through the clouds, and it reflected off something white. He had to dismount and climb a bit to reach it, and when he got there, he saw that it was a body. There were marks that indicated it had been dragged there. If Cooper had killed the man and then tried to hide his body, he had done a bad job. The body was lying with its right arm at its side and its left stretched out at an upward angle.

Locke turned the man over and saw two things. One, he'd been shot once in the heart, and two . . . it was Sheriff Mike Hammet, the lawman from Turnback Creek.

Locke sat back on his haunches and studied the matter. It was entirely possible—and probable—that the shooter on the ridge the day before had been Hammet. If he had been working with Cooper and they met up later, he probably had been shocked when Cooper shot him and left him for dead.

With the body on its back, Locke noticed an odd thing. The right hand was not only at its side, but the man's hand was in his pocket. That had to be deliberate, but for what reason? Locke decided it was to point out the fact that both arms had not been placed accidentally.

He turned the sheriff back over and placed the left arm the way it had been, at an angle. He realized that Hammet apparently had not been dead when Cooper—or whoever had killed him—had left him, and he was now pointing in the direction his killer had gone.

But had his killer, in fact, been Dale Cooper?

There was only one way to find out.

Locke went through the sheriff's pockets to see if he had anything useful. In the end, all he took was the man's gun, to have an extra. He stood up and looked around, but there was no sign of the man's horse.

He returned to his horse, mounted up, and started in the direction the dead man had been "pointing."

It was several hours later when Hoke Benson, Rome, and the rest came across the dead lawman.

"Think Locke killed him?" Eli asked.

"Why would he?" Hoke asked. "Unless the lawman was tryin' to steal the gold."

"Why not?" Rome asked. "Even a lawman can want gold."

"Instead of tin," Hoke said. He took the sheriff's badge from the dead man's shirt and pocketed it.

"Either the old marshal or Locke killed him," he said, standing up. "And if they're split up, then they're against each other."

"Who's got the gold?" Turpin asked.

"That's what we've got to find out," Hoke said.

They went back to where Bob Bailey had been holding everybody's horses.

"Any sign?" Hoke asked Rome.

"Nothing helpful."

Hoke looked up the slope.

"We got two ways we can go." He looked at Rome. "Pick one."

"Just guess?"

"Your guess is better than anyone else's."

"Then I say we keep headin' away from the mine," Rome said, pointing in the direction Locke had gone. None of these men had noticed that the sheriff had been "pointing" the way.

"Okay," Hoke said. "That's what we'll do."

"But what if they're still goin' to the mine?" Eli asked.

Hoke was tempted to tell Eli to shut his mouth, but he had a valid point.

"Okay, Eli," he said. "You take Bailey and one of the new men and keep headin' for the mine. We'll go this way."

"And if you find the gold?" Eli asked.

"We'll come back for you."

The three men exchanged glances.

"I'll stick with you," Eli said.

"Me, too," Bailey said, and the new man nodded also.

"What a world," Rome said. "Nobody trusts nobody."

"Well," Hoke said, "after all, we are tryin' to steal somebody else's gold, aren't we?"

They mounted up, and Rome took point with Hoke once again at his side.

"Why'd you take the lawman's badge?" Rome asked.

"Who knows?" Hoke replied. "It might come in handy somewhere along the way. A hunk of tin just might help us grab a bunch of gold. Wouldn't that be a hoot?"

FORTY-EIGHT

If Dale Cooper had killed Sheriff Hammet, then Locke had lost one advantage.

Cooper now had the sheriff's rifle.

Someone had steered Cooper right, as well, because the route they were on now was widening and smoothing out. There was easy passage for a buckboard. Locke just had to hope that the horses would tire from pulling all that gold.

The weather also was favoring Cooper. The sun had come out, and it didn't look as if it would rain again for some time. Of course, the weather could change abruptly in the mountains.

And fate was always ready to take a hand . . .

Locke had ridden the new trail for a few hours when the terrain started getting rocky again. It didn't slow him down at all, but it would have some effect on the buckboard. He started to wonder just when they'd get to the top of this mountain and start down the other side. Going downhill with all that weight behind them might be difficult for a tired team. Or maybe Locke was overestimating the weight of the gold, and two horses were fine pulling it all day long. It sure had been heavy when they'd loaded the crates one by one onto the buckboard. But an experienced team was used to handling freight, and Cooper might be coasting along just fine.

He topped a rise, thought he'd reached the top of the mountain, but saw that he'd been fooled. The trail did go downhill but only for a while, and then it started back up again. He could see that. But he could also see, right in the belly of the trail where it was about to start up again, Cooper and the buckboard. They had apparently gotten stuck. Cooper was out of the seat and was standing in front of the team. Maybe one of the horses had gone lame on him.

Locke quelled the urge to ride right down there on him. Perhaps if Cooper hadn't gotten the sheriff's gun, he might have. Instead, he backed his horse off so it couldn't be seen if Cooper looked up and dismounted. He dropped the horse's reins and grounded them with a large rock, then got on his belly and crawled back up to the top of the rise. He checked behind him to see if anyone was coming that way, then looked down at Cooper. The ex-marshal—and his ex-friend—had stooped down to check the horse's hooves.

Cooper lifted the horse's front leg and saw that a sharp rock apparently had sliced the animal's hoof open.

"Goddamnit," he swore, dropping the animal's leg to the ground.

He stood up and looked around him. He knew he was in the Devil's Basin, and he knew the basin's reputation. He also knew it was the quickest way off the mountain, but right now, he was in a bad spot. Right in the center of the basin, if it started to rain again—hard—he was going to be in trouble.

Cooper regretted what he had done to his friend John Locke. He regretted it, but he wouldn't have changed it if he could. Well, maybe if he could have persuaded Locke to go along with him. He underestimated Locke's honesty. He had thought—or hoped—that after all these years, Locke would be as disillusioned a man as he was and would jump at the chance to steal the gold. He'd been dead wrong. Now he hoped Locke would not come after him, because if he did, he knew he'd have to kill him in order to keep the gold.

But all of that was moot right now. He was stuck in the basin unless he could get the horses—even one that was lame—to pull him out. If he could get out of the basin and over the next rise, at least the rain would not be a problem.

Maybe if he cleaned the wound . . .

There was no way to get down to Cooper without being seen. Technically speaking, the man was in a bowl, and he was right in the center. Locke could have worked his way around to either side, but it would have taken a long time. Also, there was still no cover for him to move toward Cooper.

The buckboard was within easy rifle range, however, and if Locke called out to Cooper, he'd hear him. He squinted, trying to see where the man's rifle was. If he'd left it on the buckboard seat, then he might have the chance to get the drop on him. The problem was the buckboard and the team were between him and Cooper at the moment. He needed the man to move out into the open.

He sighted down the barrel of his rifle and waited . . .

"What's that?" Hoke Benson asked, sighting something ahead.

"Looks like a horse," Eddie Rome said.

"Yeah," Hoke said, "but whose? And what's it doin' here?"

"Looks like it's just standin' there."

The horse was actually drinking from a puddle, swishing its tail, and not doing much else.

"We need to check it out," Hoke said. "The rider might still be around."

"I'll send Turpin," Rome said.

"Let's send Bailey with him."

They turned and rode back to the other men.

"There's a horse up ahead," Hoke said. "Bob, you and Turpin go and check it out."

"We'll cover you from here," Rome said.

"Check it out?" Turpin asked.

"Ride up there, and see whose horse it is," Rome said. "Or see if it's abandoned. It might be the horse that got away from Locke and Cooper."

"What if they're still around?" Bailey asked.

"I told you," Hoke said. "We'll cover you from here."

Bailey and Turpin exchanged a glance, then separated from the rest of the men and rode forward. As Hoke, Rome, and the others watched with their rifles in their hands, they advanced closer and closer to the stray horse.

When they reached it, they exchanged words briefly, and then Bailey got down and walked to it. Meanwhile, Turpin stood in his stirrups and looked around, then waved to the others to come ahead.

When Hoke, Rome, and the others reached them, Turpin said, "Nobody around."

"Keep an eye out anyway," Hoke said. He and Rome dismounted. "What'd you find?" he asked Bailey.

"This."

He handed Hoke an envelope. It was addressed to John Locke in Las Vegas, New Mexico.

"It's Locke's horse," he said, passing the envelope to Rome.

"Maybe he's on foot," Turpin said.

"It don't matter," Hoke said. "If he's separated from Cooper and the buckboard, then there's only one man between us and the gold. We don't need to find Locke."

"What if he's on the buckboard with Cooper?" Rome asked.

"That don't matter, either," Hoke said. "We're on the right trail, boys. That gold is as good as ours."

FORTY-NINE

Locke waited patiently while Cooper checked the horses, even with the wet ground soaking through his clothes. Finally, Cooper moved away from the horses, probably planning to climb into the seat again. Locke aimed and fired one shot. It pinged off the ground in front of Cooper, and the man froze. Locke worked the lever of his rifle, and as Cooper started to take another step, he fired again, with the same result.

"John?" Cooper shouted. He had his hand on his gun, but he'd know that Locke was out of range.

"Stand fast, Coop!" Locke called out. "Where's your rifle?"

"I don't have one."

"I know you have Hammet's rifle."

Cooper didn't answer right away. "What's this about, John?" the man finally shouted. "I've been waiting for you to catch up."

"I'm sure you have," Locke called back. "Take out your gun, and toss it away as far as you can."

"If I do that, it might get damaged or go off."

"Just do it, Coop."

Cooper hesitated, then drew his pistol and tossed it. It landed with a loud clatter but did not go off.

"I don't know what you're so upset about," Cooper shouted. Both their voices echoed in that bowl.

"I'll tell you when I get down there."

"Well, come ahead," Cooper said. "I need some help with these horses, anyway."

"Lie down."

"What?"

"Facedown on the ground, Coop!"

"Come on, John—"

Locke fired another shot, which landed right at Cooper's feet and ricocheted away.

"Not as bad with a long gun as you said you were, huh, John?" Cooper called out, lying down on his face.

"Put your hands straight out from your body!"

Cooper obeyed this time without question, and Locke got to his feet and started down the slope, holding his rifle ready. He hoped Cooper wouldn't do anything foolish, because he didn't want to have to shoot the man who had been his friend for years.

When he finally reached the buckboard and the prone figure of Cooper, he saw the sheriff's carbine on the seat. He grabbed it and tossed it off into the distance, where it landed noisily. Out of nowhere, a cloud suddenly obscured the sun, and rain once again seemed imminent.

"Can I get up now?"

"Get into a seated position," Locke instructed.

"The ground is wet, John!"

"I know," Locke said. The front of his shirt and jeans were soaked. "Come on, sit."

Cooper sighed heavily and shifted into a seated position. Locke leaned against the buckboard, holding the rifle casually in his arms.

"What's this about, John?"

"You know what it's about, Coop," Locke said. "You've been lying to me from the beginning."

"About what?"

"Everything!" Locke snapped. "Your alcoholic condition, your ability with a gun, and—most of all—your intentions toward the gold."

"What intent—"

"Stealing it!" Locke said, cutting him off. "You were planning to steal this payroll right from the start. The only thing I don't understand is, why did you bring me in on it?"

"You got this wrong, John."

"I don't think so."

"Let me explain."

"Explain why you let my horse loose and left me afoot."

"I can."

"Explain why you're nowhere near the Shillstone mine."

"I took a wrong turn."

"You sure did, Coop," Locke said. "What happened to you? The law used to be everything to you."

"The law?" Cooper asked. "What did I ever get from

the law, John? You saw what they did to me in Ellsworth. I learned a new word after that. Do you know what it was? *Vilified*. Do you know what that means?"

"I know," Locke said.

"They ruined my reputation and my life," Cooper said. "Do you know what the last eight or nine years have been like for me?"

"Obviously not," Locke said. "You cut me out of your life since Ellsworth."

"Because you were there!" Cooper said. "You saw me humiliated!"

"Is that my fault?" Locke asked.

"Actually, it is," Cooper said. "I never asked you for help that day. Remember?"

"I remember," Locke said. "I also remember there were five men waiting for you at the end of the street. You might not have survived without me that day."

"That's very true, John," Cooper said. "And if I had been killed, it might not have come to this."

"This being stealing the gold, Coop?" Locke asked. "And conning me?"

"I didn't con you, John."

"Are you a drunk?"

"I was," Cooper said. "I've been a drunk for a long time, but I gave it up for this job."

"You were acting for my benefit."

"Not only yours," Cooper said. "Everybody else, too. But it backfired on me. Molly started having doubts about hiring me, so I had to bring someone else in on it, someone she'd be impressed with and trust."

"Your old friend John, huh?"

"I'm willin' to share, John," Cooper said. "I brought the subject up in Kingdom Junction, but you didn't even entertain it."

"So, you admit you intended to steal it from the beginning."

"No," he said. "Not from the beginning, but when I found how much was involved . . ."

"And you needed another man to help with the gold."

"That happened afterward," Cooper said. "Even after I sent you that telegram. I didn't find out till later that the payroll was gonna be in gold. That sort of put a crimp in my plan, having to use a buckboard and all."

"So you intended simply to ride off with the payroll."

"Start up the mountain on horseback, and just keep going."

"When did you recruit the sheriff?"

"After I found out about the gold," Cooper said. "I read him right from the beginning. I knew that the gold would persuade him to help me."

"You needed him to get you away from me."

"Right."

"And you planned on killing him all along."

Cooper didn't respond right away, then said, "I could tell you it was self-defense, that he tried to take the gold for himself."

"But that's not the way it happened, is it?"

"No."

"So, you killed him in cold blood."

"Yes."

"You should have made sure he was dead, Coop," Locke said. "He pointed me right to you."

"I was wonderin' how you caught up to me—although if one of the horses hadn't come up lame . . ."

"I still would have caught up with you," Locke said. "No matter how long it took."

"Come on, John," Cooper said. "There's a lot of gold there. We just have to get over this mountain, and we're home free."

"And how do you intend to do that with a lame horse?"

"I assume you still have a horse."

"Actually, I found yours."

"There you go," Cooper said. "We just hook that one up to the buckboard, and we're on our way."

"And how long before you try to kill me for the gold, Coop?"

"I wouldn't do that, John," Cooper said. "You're my friend."

"That didn't stop you from conning me and leaving me on foot."

"But I knew you'd survive," Cooper said. "I'd never kill you. I'm not that far gone."

"Seems to me you've gone as far as you can, Coop," Locke said. "Killing a lawman sent you over the edge."

"And you've never killed a lawman?"

"Never."

"Well . . . gold, John," Cooper said. This seemed to be the only argument left to him now. "Eighty thousand in gold, split two ways."

"No deal, Coop."

"What do you intend to do?"

"Deliver the gold to the mine," Locke said, "and you to the law."

"There ain't no more law in Turnback Creek."

"Then we'll go to Kingdom Junction," Locke said. "I'll turn you over to Sheriff Maddox."

"Maddox," Cooper said, shaking his head. "He'd come in for a quarter of the gold, John. I could smell it on him."

"By the time I turn you over to him, the miners will have the gold," Locke said.

Cooper shook his head again. "I can't let you do that, John," he said. "I have too many plans for the gold."

"Then we have a problem here, Coop."

"More problems than you know, John."

It took a moment for Locke to notice that Cooper was looking up the slope as he said this.

FIFTY

When Hoke Benson, Eddie Rome, and their men came across the second horse, they saw that the reins had been grounded and knew they were in luck.

"Somebody's around here someplace," Rome said, looking around.

"Let's spread out," Hoke said, dismounting. "Anybody sees anybody, don't sing out. Don't let them know you seen them. Just come and get the rest of us."

Everyone nodded.

Hoke and Rome stayed together and approached the horse.

"Rifle's still here," Hoke said.

"Don't mean nothin'," Rome said. "The sheriff's rifle was gone, remember?"

"That's right," Hoke said. "The sheriff's horse is on this mountain someplace. Heck, maybe this is it."

"Well, whoever was riding it is around here," Rome

said. "He grounded those reins. Let's see what's up ahead."

The two men moved forward cautiously to the top of the rise, and suddenly they were looking down into a basin at two men and a buckboard of gold.

"I know this place," Rome said.

"What?"

"The Devil's Basin, they call it," he said.

"Why?" Hoke asked.

Rome hesitated, then said, "I don't remember. I just know I heard of it."

"Well," Hoke said, "whatever it's called, there's our gold."

"And them two don't look like friends," Rome said.

One man was standing and holding a rifle, while the other was sitting on his ass.

"Let's get the others," Hoke said. "We got 'em now, Rome. We got 'em, and we got our gold."

They retreated and found the rest of their men.

"Let's mount up," Hoke said. "I want them to see us at full strength."

"You thinkin' they might just walk away and leave the gold?" Rome asked. "Without a fight?"

"I didn't think so before, but maybe," Hoke said. "Maybe they will. Why don't we just let 'em see us and find out?"

FIFTY-ONE

When Locke looked up, he saw seven mounted men at the top of the slope. He cursed himself for having left his horse up there.

"Looks like we're gonna need each other, John," Cooper said. "We can take up our argument another time."

Locke knew he was in no position to take any other stance. "Coop," he said, "stand up and move real slow to get your guns."

Cooper got to his feet. "I hope they let me get that far," he said.

"How bad is that horse?"

"He cut the bottom of his foot pretty bad," Cooper said. "What are they doin'? They're just sittin' there."

"They're showing us their strength," Locke said, "and, hopefully, giving you time to get to your guns."

The pistol and rifle had been tossed in the same direction. The rifle, being heavier, had not gone as far, and that was the weapon Locke and Cooper wanted the most.

Locke held his breath the closer Cooper got to it.

"What's he doin'?" Hoke asked as Cooper moved across the floor of the basin.

"I can't see . . . wait," Rome said. "He's tryin' to get to his guns. See that rifle?"

"That's Cooper," Hoke said. "The other one is Locke. Looks like Locke had the drop on the old marshal."

"I can pick him off from here," Turpin said, raising his rifle.

"No," Hoke said. "Let the old man get to his rifle."

"Why?" Rome asked.

"Why not?" Hoke said. "They're outnumbered seven to two, and they have no cover. What are they gonna do?"

"They did okay when they were outnumbered five to two," Rome said. "Remember?"

"I remember," Hoke said. "But this is different. This time, we got 'em."

Cooper reached his rifle and his pistol, too, which he holstered as he joined Locke by the buckboard.

"They figure they've got us," Locke said. "That's why they let you get to your guns."

"Why don't they make a move?"

"Why should they?" Locke asked. "Where are we going to go?"

"They don't know we have a lame horse."

"If we try to leave with the gold, they'll either start

shooting or rush us. On the other hand, if we just try to leave without the gold, I bet they'd let us go."

"Why would we do that?"

"To save our lives?"

"I'm not leavin' without that gold, John," Cooper said. "I've got no life without it."

"Why should I stay here and fight for it, then," Locke asked, "if you're going to take it?"

"I told you before," Cooper said. "For half."

"I don't want half, Coop," Locke said. "I don't even want it all."

"You won't leave."

"Why not?"

"Because that's not the kind of man you are," Cooper said. "Because these are the kinds of odds you like."

"Seven to two," Locke said. "How much worse could it get?"

At that moment, the sky opened up, and it started to pour.

FIFTY-TWO

I t was a deluge.

It was raining so hard no one could see. It was as if all of the rain that week had been leading up to this. Creek beds and mountain streams overflowed quickly from the runoff at the top of the mountain, and tons of water started down.

"I can't see a damned thing!" Hoke yelled.

The rain was falling with such force that the sound of it was deafening.

Rome leaned over and shouted into Hoke's ear, "I remember why they call this Devil's Basin!"

"Why?"

" 'Cause it fills up like a son of a bitch when it rains!" Rome said. "They're gonna drown, and we can just go down and get the gold."

"But the gold will be underwater, won't it?"

"The basin drains almost as fast as it fills when it stops rainin'," Rome said.

"So, all we gotta do is wait out the rain?"

"Right," Rome said. "It should do our work for us."

"What if they try to leave during the storm?"

"My guess is they have a lame horse," Rome said. "That's why they were down there in the first place."

Their horses were starting to get skittish from the rain.

"We've got to move these horses back and calm them down," Rome said. "We have to make sure we don't end up afoot."

"Let's do it, then," Hoke replied.

As they started to lead their horses back from the edge of the basin, something suddenly bolted past them.

"What was that?" Hoke yelled.

"It was that other horse," Rome said. "It's runnin' down there to drown with them."

"Let's get our horses to safety," Hoke shouted.

Locke and Cooper had taken shelter beneath the buckboard, but they were already up to their shins in water. The water was running down from both sides of the basin, but not from where the road led in and out.

"We could get away if we could get up this road," Cooper said. "Maybe the horses will be frightened enough to move, even the one with a bad hoof."

"We'd never make it," Locke said.

"We can't stay here," Cooper said. "We'll drown. This basin fills up fast when it rains like this."

"You knew about this?" Locke demanded.

Cooper nodded. "I was warned not to come this way," he said. "It's called the Devil's Basin."

"And for good reason, obviously," Locke said. "We have to get out from under here."

The water was knee deep, and they could no longer remain under the buckboard.

"I can't see up the slope," Cooper said, "but I hear something."

They both looked up. Visibility was nil, but suddenly a horse burst into view, eyes wide and nostrils flaring. It was flailing about in the knee-deep water, unsure which way to go.

"That's my horse!" Cooper said.

"He got loose," Locke shouted. "Grab him, and get the saddle off. I have an idea."

While Cooper grabbed his horse, Locke went to the team and unhitched the lame horse. Cooper brought his mount over without the saddle, and they hooked it up to the buckboard.

They scrambled into the buckboard. Locke grabbed the reins and flicked them at the frightened horses. The lame horse had already wandered its way up the slope and out of sight. The other two, however, were not used to being a team. They were not pulling together, and the weight of the gold in the water was holding them back.

"We should mount them and ride out," Locke said.

"I'm not leavin' the gold!" Cooper shouted.

"It'll be at the bottom of the basin, in the water," Locke said. "They won't be able to get to it."

"The basin drains as fast as it fills, once the rain stops," Cooper said. "At least, that's what I've heard."

"Damn it, Coop."

"Go ahead and leave," Cooper said. "I'm stayin'."

"Our guns are wet, and so are theirs." Locke tried again. "If they come down here, we can't fight them off."

"I tol' you, go ahead and leave!"

"You're still a stubborn old mule," Locke said. "I've got another idea."

"Let's hear it."

Locke told it to the ex-lawman, who listened intently. "That's still leavin' the gold."

"Not if they go for it," Locke said. "If they think we got away with it, they won't come down here or even wait for it to drain. They'll just look for a way around so they can get back on our trail."

Cooper was unsure.

"If we stay much longer, Coop," Locke said, "we'll drown."

"All right, damn it!" Cooper said. "Let's try it."

They both got in the back of the buckboard and started unloading the gold.

FIFTY-THREE

With the weight on the buckboard lessened, even the mismatched team was able to pull it out of the basin. Once they reached the top of the slope opposite the seven men, they stopped. They couldn't see anyone, and no one could see them.

Since they were out of the water, they were able to get out of the rain by crawling back beneath the buckboard. They hobbled the horses so they couldn't drag the thing right over them.

"This better work," Cooper said. "If I lose that gold—"

"I don't want to lose it any more than you do, Coop," Locke said, cutting him off.

"Yeah, but for different reasons."

"The right reasons."

"Right for who? At my age, John," Cooper said, "I'm only concerned with what's right for me."

"Well, I've heard that about old folks, Coop," Locke said. "They get real selfish . . . and cranky."

"I'm cranky because I'm wet," Cooper said. "Bein' old's got nothin' to do with it."

The ground was soaked, with water running beneath them. They tried sitting on the one slicker they had, but it did little to help. All they were really able to do was clean their weapons and then keep them dry. When the rain stopped, they were going to need them.

"I guess this is the big storm Molly said was coming," Locke said. "If you knew about this basin, why did you ever come this way?"

"It's the shortest way over the mountain," Cooper said. "How was I to know I'd get stuck right at the bottom of it?"

"Fate," Locke said.

"What?"

"It was fate that you got stuck there, so I could catch up to you."

"It was a bad break, that's all," Cooper said. "After we're finished with these men, we still have our own business to finish. I'm still takin' this gold, John. I deserve it."

"The miners have worked for it, not you, Coop."

"Bullshit!" Cooper said. "I worked real hard for it, believe me. And I'm still gonna work harder, thanks to this plan of yours."

"At least we know no one will get to the gold for a while," Locke said. "How fast did you say the basin drains once the rain stops?"

"I don't know," Cooper said. "I just heard stories. I never expected to have to time it."

Locke was starting to wonder if the rain would ever stop.

The rain stopped at night, so even without the driving downpour, they couldn't see anything.

"What if they're sneakin' up on us in the dark?" Cooper asked.

"They're not moving, Coop," Locke said. "They couldn't see through the rain, and now they can't see in the dark. There are still clouds, and they're blocking the moon. Don't worry, when the sun comes up, we'll be here, and they'll be all the way on the other side. It will take them hours to work their way around."

"And what will we be doing in the meantime?"

"Getting ready for them."

When morning broke, the seven men got to their feet and looked down at the basin. It was more than half filled with water.

"I thought you said it drained quick," Hoke said to Rome accusingly. He pointed his finger. "It stopped raining halfway through the night, and there's still a ton of water down there."

"I don't know," Rome said with a shrug. "That's just what I heard."

"Where's the buckboard?" Turpin asked.

"It's underwater," Eli said. "They're all underwater."

"I don't think so," Bailey said.

They all looked at him.

"What are you talkin' about?" Hoke asked.

Bailey pointed, and they all looked. They saw across the basin from them the buckboard, with two men standing next to it.

"What the hell?" Rome said.

"They got out?" Hoke said.

"Looks like," Rome said.

"But why didn't they just leave?"

"In that downpour?" Rome asked. "They couldn't see any better than we could."

"Well, they can see now." Hoke's tone was still accusatory as he glared at Rome.

"And so can we," Rome said.

"Hey," Sharp said. "What are they doin'?"

They all turned their eyes to the two men across the basin again.

"They're holdin' somethin' up in their hands," Hoke said.

"Somethin' shiny," Turpin said, squinting his eyes.

"Whadda they got that's shiny?" Eli asked.

The seven stared at the two, who were both holding something over their heads that reflected the sun.

"Gold," Rome said.

"What?" Hoke asked.

"They're holding gold over their heads," Rome said.

"The bastards have our gold!" Turpin said.

He raised his rifle to fire. Rome shouted, "No!" but Turpin pulled the trigger, then levered another round into the chambers and fired again. Four other men started firing, and then Rome saw Hoke firing angrily as well and figured . . . what the hell.

FIFTY-FOUR

Locke and Cooper scampered for cover as bullets began to whiz past them, striking the back of the buckboard.

"We've got to move the horses before they get hit," Locke shouted.

They both ran to the head of the team and quickly walked them away from the edge and down out of sight.

"I guess they saw the gold," Cooper said.

"Yeah," Locke said, dropping the two handfuls of gold coins he had been holding into one of the empty crates. "Luckily, they don't know that we only have two handfuls each."

"What do you think they'd do if they knew the rest of it was underwater?" Cooper asked.

"They'd probably dive in after it," Locke said. "But nobody's got any hope of getting to those coins until that basin drains."

"And who knows when that'll be?" Cooper asked.

"I thought you did," Locke said, "but I was wrong."

"I told you," Cooper responded, "I only know what I heard."

"Well, I guess we're going to find out for sure."

Across the basin, all the men except Hoke Benson and Eddie Rome were panicking.

"They got our gold," Eli cried.

"They used the cover of the rain, and the night, to get it out of the basin," Hoke said. "They must have hitched that stray horse to the buckboard."

"That means they've got a mismatched team," Rome said. "Horses in teams work together, and they don't like it when strange horses are next to them. They'll have some trouble for a while. That'll slow them down."

"We have to work our way around to the other side and pick up their trail," Hoke said.

"Why don't we go across?" Turpin asked.

"The water level is too deep, so shut up, Roy."

"I thought you said it drains fast," Eli said.

"Not that fast," Rome replied. "We can't afford to wait. They'll get too far ahead of us."

"Let's go," Hoke said. "We can push the horses, because they've had a long rest, thanks to the rain."

"When do we get to eat?" Bailey asked.

"When we get the gold," Hoke said, "we'll eat."

He and Rome mounted up, and the rest followed. Eli reached into his saddlebags and brought out a hunk of beef jerky.

"Here, Bob," he said. "Chew on that."

"Thanks."

Some of the others reached out and grabbed some jerky as well, chewing on it as they followed their two leaders.

Locke and Cooper were on their bellies, peering across the basin while trying to avoid being seen themselves.

"I think they rode off," Cooper said.

"Let's give it some time," Locke said. "It'll take them hours to work their way around."

Cooper looked at Locke. "If the basin doesn't drain quickly, what do we do? If we wait here, we'll have to face the seven of them when they reach us."

"Well," Locke said, "one of us could take the buckboard and lead them away."

"While the other one stays here with the gold?" Cooper asked. "I'm for that. I'll stay with the gold."

"I don't think so, Coop."

"Even if I could get down there to it, how would I get away with it?" Cooper asked.

"I wouldn't put it past you to have another accomplice trailing us," Locke said. "No, I'll stay with the gold, and you lead them away."

"Not a chance."

"I don't have an accomplice trailing us," Locke said, "if that's what you're worried about."

"I'm not letting that gold out of my sight."

"Well, it's out of your sight now, Coop," Locke pointed out. "It's underwater."

"It'll be there when the water drains."

"Maybe."

Looking alarmed, Cooper asked, "What does that mean?"

"Well . . . when it was in the wooden chests, it was pretty heavy, but I don't know if each individual coin will be able to resist the current, depending on just how quickly the water does drain."

Cooper turned to face Locke. "Why didn't you bring that up before?"

"This was the only plan I had," Locke said. "So far, it looks like it's worked pretty well."

"So far?" Cooper asked. "You wouldn't really care if the coins drained out with the water, would you? Just so long as I don't end up with the gold."

"We'll just have to wait for the basin to drain out to find out for sure, won't we?"

"And manage to fight off seven gunmen with gold fever."

"Oh, yeah," Locke said. "That, too."

FIFTY-FIVE

They were still faced with the prospect of the seven men working their way around the basin before the basin could drain, giving them the chance to recover the gold. If the gold coins drained away with the water, Locke would have to explain it to Molly. But Cooper was right about one thing. Locke would have preferred that the gold be lost so that Cooper wouldn't get it. That would be small consolation to Molly and to the miners waiting to get paid.

"Okay," Locke said after an hour of watching the basin. "I have another idea."

"Let's hear it."

"We both get on the buckboard and get out of here," he said. "We lead them away from here and then double back."

"What if there's nowhere on the trail to double back?"

"We'll have to take that chance," Locke said. "We can't

let them find us here with empty crates, waiting for the water to drain."

Cooper cast a forlorn look at the water. "What if it drains and someone comes along and finds all that gold?" he complained.

"No one's going to find it, Coop," Locke said. "There's nobody just riding around up here. Anyone up here is already looking for the gold."

"What if there are other men?"

"Coop, we've got to do something. We can't just sit here and wait for them."

Cooper suddenly brightened. "Maybe we'll find some-place along the way we can ambush them."

"I'm not shooting anybody in the back, Coop," Locke said. "Not even them."

"I didn't say anything about shootin' anybody in the back, did I?" Cooper demanded. "We get the drop on them, we can take their weapons and their horses. Leave them on foot."

"Let's get moving, then," Locke said. "We've got to get these two horses to work together."

Locke moved to the buckboard and climbed into the seat. Cooper gave one more morose look to the water-filled basin, with the gold coins languishing at the bottom, then turned and followed.

The horses eventually came to some sort of mutual understanding, and they were able to get under way. Once they got away from the basin, the road widened and continued up, but then suddenly it peaked, and they were on their way down.

"Let's not go too far down," Cooper said. "We just have to come back up again."

"Looks like plenty of places for an ambush now," Locke said, studying the terrain.

They had their pick of rocks and clumps of trees and bushes on this side of the mountain.

"Should we leave the buckboard out in the open to bait them, do ya think?" Cooper asked.

"No," Locke said. "They'll think something's up. Let's find someplace we can hide it completely and then find some high ground from where we can get the drop on them."

"Okay."

They found a stand of trees that actually had a clearing inside it. They had to force the horses to push their way through while pulling the buckboard along with them.

"Now, if the horses will be quiet, we'll be fine," Locke said.

"That's if they come this way."

"They'll come," Locke said. "To have followed us this far, they have to have a pretty good tracker with them. They'll come."

"Then let's find that high ground," Cooper said. "You on one side, me on the other. We'll get them in a cross-fire."

"Coop," Locke said warningly, "no firing unless they force our hand. I mean it."

"But there's seven of 'em!"

"If we get the drop on them, we'll control them," Locke said. "They've got to have a leader they'll follow. Not like those storekeepers we killed. If we have to kill one, it can be the leader. I don't want to kill seven more men unless it's necessary."

"What makes you think these ain't just a bunch of store-keepers, too?" Cooper asked.

"Well, for one thing, I already said they must have a good tracker with them," Locke said. "For the other, they shot pretty good back there. They almost took our heads off, remember?"

"All the more reason—"

"Coop," Locke said, "if you start shooting and I don't think it was necessary, I'm going to let you face them on your own. I won't fire a goddamn shot!"

"You wouldn't."

"I would," Locke said, "and I'll go back for the gold."

Cooper frowned, trying to figure a way out of this argu-ment, but he couldn't. "You drive a hard bargain, John."

"Are we agreed?"

"We're agreed."

"Then let's find that high ground."

FIFTY-SIX

"Wait." Hoke Benson held up his hand to stop the progress of himself and the six men with him. "What is it?" he asked Eddie Rome.

Rome didn't answer right away, just cocked his head. He was either listening or thinking—maybe both. "Somethin's wrong."

"What?"

"I don't know," Rome said. "It just doesn't feel right."

They had reached the other side of the basin and paused to look down at the water.

"Not drainin' fast," Hoke said. "Good thing we went around."

It wasn't hard for Rome to track them from there. There was only one trail leading away from the basin. When the trail widened and the terrain began to offer more hiding places, Rome became cautious. Unfortunately, his caution had to be tempered with the impatience of the other men.

Eli Jordan leaned over and said to Bob Bailey, "They're gonna keep gettin' farther and farther away the more careful Rome gets."

Hoke turned around and gave Eli a hard look.

"Eli, you and Bailey want to ride up ahead and check things out?" he asked.

"That's okay, Hoke," Eli said, shaking his head. "We'll ride along with everybody else."

"Eddie?"

Rome looked at Hoke. "Could be a trap."

"Can we go around?" Hoke asked.

"I don't know enough about these mountains to say."

"Okay," Hoke said. "We'll go in single file from here, spread out. If a trap gets sprung, we won't all be in it."

"Two men are gonna set a trap for seven?" Roy Turpin said. "It don't make sense."

"It makes perfect sense," Hoke said.

Rome turned and said, "You saw those two men handle five pretty easily out in the open. From cover, they could take most of us out before we know what's happenin'."

"I'm just sayin'—"

"You say too much, Roy," Rome said. "Shut up."

"Eli," Hoke said, "you and Turpin take the lead, and we'll string out behind you."

"Hoke—"

"Do it!"

Eli looked at Bailey, who shrugged and looked away. Eli then looked at Turpin, and the two men rode ahead.

* * *

Locke noticed immediately that the seven men were riding toward them in single file, pretty well strung out. This would make it difficult to get the drop on all seven at one time.

Locke and Cooper had found rock formations they could climb to get to high ground, and they were able to see not only the approaching men but also each other. Locke tried gesturing to Cooper, attempting to wave him off. He wanted to let the seven men pass without incident. If that happened, they'd be able to double back to the basin.

If Cooper did not get his message and opened fire, they were going to be at a distinct disadvantage, despite having higher ground. Locke hoped that Cooper was still enough of an experienced lawman to realize this and let them pass.

Locke crouched down, now out of sight of the men and of Cooper. He waited tensely, not knowing what Cooper was going to do. Despite what he'd said, there was no way he'd leave his friend—or ex-friend—to face the seven men alone. If Cooper opened fire, there was definitely going to be a bloodbath.

One by one, the men passed Locke's position. He could tell from their hunched shoulders that they were probably waiting for something to happen. Once the seventh man went past, Locke breathed a sigh of relief and started climbing down from his position.

Hoke rode up next to Rome and said, "No ambush."

"Not there," Rome said, "but it could still happen

somewhere up ahead. I suggest we keep ridin' this way, single file."

"You heard the man," Hoke snapped at the others. "Single file!"

Locke met up with Cooper by the buckboard. "You got my signal," he said.

"You were waving frantically enough," Cooper said. "Not that you needed to. I could see how stretched out they were. We were better off lettin' them go by. Now we can double back and pick up the gold."

"If the basin has drained."

"There's only one way to find out," Cooper said.

"Let's just hope they go a long way before they realize we doubled back," Locke said.

"Jesus!" Cooper said.

The sun had come out and was shining so brightly that the piles of gold coins at the bottom of the water-filled basin were practically glowing. The water, having run off from the tops of the mountains, was crystal clear, and they could plainly see the gold gleaming beneath it.

"We can't leave it there!" Cooper said. "Someone will see it."

Locke didn't bother arguing that nobody traveled this way by accident. He had argued that already. They did have to do something, though, because the water was not draining as quickly as they would have liked, and if the seven men did double back, they'd know in an instant it was there.

"I got another question."

"What's that?"

"Once we have all four crates filled and put back on the buckboard, where do we go?"

"Well, I know where I want to go," Locke said.

"And I know where I want to go," Cooper said.

"But there's seven men that way, and they may be coming back at any time," Locke said.

"Shit!"

"We'll deal with that question once we have the gold back on the buckboard. Okay?"

"Okay."

Locke was able to walk down to the water's edge, dragging two crates with him. He walked out into the water until he was waist deep, then discovered how buoyant the empty crates were. He could not get two of them submerged at the same time. In fact, he couldn't get one of them underwater. He walked back up to where Cooper was waiting by the buckboard. At this point, he was already numb from the cold.

"I need something heavy to weight each crate down. Once I get them submerged, I can substitute the coins for it."

"How about your gun?"

"How about your gun?" Locke asked. Neither of them wanted to be defenseless before the other. "No, forget it. One gun won't do it."

"Won't it sink when it's filled with water?"

Locke stared at Cooper and felt stupid. He'd fought with the crates trying to get them underwater but had not held one down long enough for it to fill. "I'll try that."

He took both crates back to the water's edge, waded out as far as he could, then held one down until it filled with water. It sank to the bottom like a stone. He waved to Cooper, filled the other, and watched it sink. Then he held his breath and submerged himself.

He had to drag the crates along the bottom until he got to the gold. By that time, he needed a breath, so he swam to the top, took another breath, and then went back down. It was only a matter of a few more feet, and he would simply have been able to wade to the gold, but they didn't have time to wait for that much more water to drain.

While he was underwater, filling the crates with gold coins, he tried not to think about what he'd do if he came back to the surface and saw the seven men there. There was always the chance they'd come back. If they caught him in the water, he was as good as dead.

When he had one chest filled, he swam to the surface for the rope. He dove with it, tied it around one chest, then went back for the other and did the same. Once both chests were tied, he signaled Cooper to have the horses pull. While the horses dragged the chests from the water, he got the other two chests and started repeating the process.

Next time he came to the surface, he waved, and Cooper waved at him to come out. Locke waded out and climbed up to where Cooper was standing. When he got there, he could hear the horses breathing hard and knew something was wrong.

"What's wrong?"

"They need a rest," Cooper said. "The crates filled with gold and water were too heavy. Once they got them out, though, the water drained out, and it got easier. Still, pulling the buckboard and the crates has exhausted them—not to mention fighting each other."

"We've already been here too long," Locke said. It was midday now, and the sun was directly above them, about to begin its descent. It was getting colder, and Locke was having trouble feeling his feet and legs. He hoped he wouldn't end up losing any toes. "If they come back, we're dead."

"If I push the horses," Cooper said, "they won't be any use to us once the buckboard is loaded."

That was true.

"All right," Locke said. "We'll rest them, but we better keep watch for those men."

"Agreed."

"We've been had," Rome said.

"What?"

"They doubled back on us."

"How could they have?" Hoke asked.

"There have been a few places they could have hidden a buckboard," Rome said. "Not many, but a few."

"Are you sure?"

"I'm seeing no sign at all," Rome said. "They could not have passed by here without leavin' some sign."

"So we gotta go back up the mountain."

"Yep."

Hoke turned in his saddle and looked back at the other five men behind them. "We're turnin' around!"

They split the watch while the horses rested. After giving the animals as long as they dared, they tied another crate. They decided to bring the last two up one at a time and to help the horses by pulling on the rope themselves—at least, until the water drained from the crates.

By the time they got the crates up, the horses were breathing hard again, but not like before. They rested the animals while they loaded each crate onto the buckboard one at a time. By this time, they were both huffing and puffing as much as the horses.

"Did we lose any coins?" Cooper asked.

"I didn't stop to count."

"Well, did you get them all?"

"I think so."

They looked down into the water. The sun was going down and was at the wrong angle. If there were any coins left at the bottom, they were not reflecting the light. They were left to guess.

"You could go back down and check."

"If I missed any," Locke said, "it was only one or two. I'm not going back down. I'm getting dressed, and we're getting out of here."

"Which way are we going?"

"Back," Locke said. "We can't go forward—we'll run into them for sure. We've got to go back."

"We can go to that clearing again."

"We might run into them first, Coop," Locke said. "We

have to go back. We'll work our way around this basin and head back."

"To town?"

"To the mine."

Cooper backed away from Locke, his hand hovering above his gun. Locke had pulled on his underwear, jeans, and boots, had donned his shirt but not buttoned it yet, but had not yet retrieved his gun belt from the seat of the buckboard.

"I ain't givin' up that gold, John," Cooper said. "I just ain't."

Locke looked into Cooper's eyes and then down at the single eye of the man's gun. Both seemed to mean business. He was no longer sure about ex-Marshal Dale Cooper, and he had no idea whether or not the man would actually shoot him.

But he knew that the seven men who had just appeared a hundred yards away would.

"Coop—"

Cooper looked and saw the mounted men.

"We'll finish this later," he said. "Better get to your guns."

FIFTY-EIGHT

"Why'd they come back here?" Turpin asked aloud, staring at the two men next to the buckboard.

"There was nowhere else to go," Hoke said. "Doubling back had to bring them here."

"And maybe . . ." Rome said.

"Maybe what?" Hoke asked.

Rome hesitated, then said, "Maybe the payroll was still here all along."

"What? Where?" Hoke demanded.

"In the water . . . maybe."

"Wha—goddamnit!" Hoke took a deep breath. "Never mind. We're here now, so are they, and so is the gold."

"So, what do we do now?" Eli asked.

"We take it," Hoke said.

Locke ran to the buckboard to grab his rifle and hand-gun. He strapped the belt on quickly, tossed Cooper his rifle, and picked up his own. Cooper came to join him by the buckboard.

"This is the only cover we have," he said. "If they charge us, we can get several of them before they reach us."

"If they charge us," Locke said. "They have no cover where they are. Let's see how they want to play it."

"Let's rush 'em," Turpin said.

"Most of us would be dead before we reached them," Rome said. "We have no cover."

"Dismount," Hoke said.

"What?"

"Dismount, now!"

All seven men dismounted.

"Keep the horses between them and us," Hoke said, "until I decide what to do."

"Good thinkin'," Rome said. "What *are* we gonna do?"

Hoke took a moment, then said, "I'll talk to them, give them a chance to walk away."

"Why do that?" Eli asked. "Why don't we just kill them?"

"They have cover," Rome said. "We don't."

"They'll kill you," Eli said.

"They'll listen," Hoke said, taking out a white handkerchief.

"Damn it," Cooper said. "They're using their horses as cover."

"We might be able to use that to our advantage," Locke said, getting an idea.

"Like how?"

"Wait," Locke said. "Somebody's waving a white flag. They want to talk."

"Locke! Cooper! I want to talk."

"I should put a bullet in his—" Cooper started, but Locke cut him off.

"Let's see what he has to say."

"We could kill him."

"That would only reduce the odds by one," Locke said. "Let's listen to what he has to say."

"Fine," Cooper said. To the man with the white flag, he shouted, "Go ahead and talk!"

The spokesman came out from behind the horses, still holding his white flag.

"That's close enough," Cooper said when the man got to within about fifty feet. "We can hear you fine."

"My name's Benson," the man said. "Hoke Benson."

"Never heard of you," Cooper said.

"Don't matter," Hoke said. "I'm givin' you both a chance to walk away and leave the gold."

"No," Cooper said.

"Don't you want to discuss it?"

"There's no need to discuss it," Locke said. "We're not walking away from the gold."

Hoke stared at them, then shook his head. "You're outnumbered and outgunned."

"That's okay," Cooper said.

"You'll die," the man said. "Both of you."

"So will you," Locke said. "Some of you."

"But the survivors will get the gold," Hoke said, "and that won't be either of you."

"Will it be you?" Cooper asked.

Hoke Benson said, "That's the plan. That's been the plan all along."

"Do your men know that?" Locke asked.

"They know what I tell them."

"What if we tell them your big plan?" Cooper asked.

"They won't believe you."

"You better go back to them, then," Locke said, "and see if they're willing to die so you can have the gold."

"I gave you a chance," Hoke said. "Nobody can say I didn't. Think it over. I'll come back in five minutes."

Hoke turned and walked back to his men. Cooper was tempted to shoot him in the back, but he knew Locke would not go for that.

"So, what do we do now?" Cooper asked.

"Wait for him to come back, and then tell him no again."

"And then what?"

"I've got an idea."

Cooper looked at him. "What?"

Quickly, Locke explained what he had in mind.

"That's not very fair," Cooper finally said.

"I know."

Cooper smiled. "I love it."

"What'd they say?" Eli asked when Hoke returned.

"What I thought they'd say," he answered. "No."

"So, let's take 'em."

"No," Hoke said. "I gave them five minutes to think it over."

"Why?" Rome asked.

"The old man," Hoke said. "He looks worn out. I think he's the weak link. The job was his, and he brought Locke in on it, so I think he's callin' the shots."

"And?" Rome asked.

"He might decide to walk away. Let's wait and see."

Hoke had no idea that he'd completely misread the entire situation.

Five minutes later, under the cover of the white flag, Hoke walked back out.

"No," Cooper said.

"Pity," Hoke replied, shaking his head. "You ol' boys could have lived to a ripe old age."

"What fun would that be?" Cooper asked.

"You knew we'd refuse, Benson," Locke said. "This is all just an act for your men."

Hoke's smile broadened, and he said, "Smart Widow-maker."

"Let's kill him now," Cooper said.

"Yes," Locke said. "Let's."

"You can't," Hoke said, waving his white flag at them. "That wouldn't be fair."

"I'd rather be unfair and alive," Locke said, "than fair and dead. Wouldn't you, Coop?"

"Definitely."

"You . . . you wouldn't . . ." Hoke said, realizing for the first time that he might have made a mistake. "You're . . . you're lawmen."

"I don't see any badges on our chests," Locke said.

Hoke considered turning and running back to his men, but he knew he'd never make it. He had only one choice, and it was his own damn fault. He should have sent Rome out to talk to them.

He went for his gun, and both Locke and Cooper shot him.

FIFTY-NINE

"Jesus!" Eli said. "They shot down Hoke!"

"They're crazy!" Bailey said.

Bently and Sharp, the two newest men in the group, didn't react as violently. They hadn't known Hoke as long as Eli and Bailey.

"Damn," Rome said, but mostly out of admiration for what the two men had done.

"Eddie," Turpin said, "whadda we do?"

"Do we still want the gold?" Rome asked.

"I want it," Turpin said.

Rome looked at Bently and Sharp. "You fellas?"

"Equal shares?" Bently asked.

"Equal."

"We're in," Sharp said.

Now Rome looked at Eli and Bailey.

"I dunno . . ." Bailey said.

"Jeez," Eli said. "They killed Hoke." He was still

in shock. After all, Hoke made all the decisions . . .

"You fellas can't make up your own minds?" Rome said.

Both men just stared at him.

"Okay," Rome said, ignoring them. "Let's take 'em."

"They're startin' to mount up," Cooper said. "They're gonna rush us."

"Then let's do it. The horses," Locke said. He dropped into a crouch and raised his rifle. Cooper followed, and they started firing. At this range, they couldn't miss something as big as a horse.

Of course, Locke's idea was much more than just shooting Hoke Benson and the horses. The six men who were left were standing in the midst of seven animals weighing more than a thousand pounds each—and horses were skittish, didn't like loud noises . . . like gunshots.

Firing into their midst would panic the heck out of them.

Eli and Bently started to mount, but before they could, hot lead struck both their horses, and the animals went down. Eli's horse fell right on him, pinning him from the waist down. He screamed and thrashed about as the horse's weight crushed his legs. As the two horses fell, a bullet smashed into Bailey's chest, knocking him onto his back.

"Jesus!" Rome shouted, surprised by the attack. "Shoot back!"

The horses, smelling the two dead beasts and hearing the sound of the shots, began to panic. If the men had been able to get mounted, they still might have controlled their horses and rushed Locke and Cooper, but the two men never stopped firing, putting their pistols and extra guns to use as well, and the horses started to go mad. One horse kicked Eli in the head as he struggled beneath his animal, splitting his skull and, mercifully, killing him. That horse and another ran off. Bently was able to mount his horse, but his intention was to run, not fight. As he urged his horse in the opposite direction, the panicked animal stumbled and fell. Bently was thrown and landed with enough impact to break his neck.

Sharp and Rome were still fighting their horses, yanking on their reins, trying to get control, while another animal went down beneath the barrage of bullets. There was so much chaos that Locke and Cooper had time to reload, and they continued to fire while advancing on foot.

Rome saw the two men coming toward them, released his horse and went for his gun. At that moment, a bullet struck his hip, shattering it. He screamed and went down.

Sharp, seeing that he was the last man standing, released his horse, threw his hands into the air, and starting shouting, "Hey, hey, wait, wait, wait . . ."

Cooper shot him.

When they reached the fallen party, Locke checked the men and found all but Rome dead. He was amazed that he and Cooper had managed to kill only half of them, while the horses—driven mad by the noise, and the smell of blood and death—had done the rest.

Three horses were dead. He felt bad about that. The surviving animals had run off, and Rome was rolling around on the ground holding his hip. When he saw

Locke and Cooper approaching him, he reached for his fallen gun, but Cooper stepped on his arm to stop him.

"Not fair . . ." he muttered, staring up at the two men.

"What did you think we would do?" Cooper asked. "Wait for you to rush us? Fight fair? The graveyards are full of men who fought fair."

"W-White flag . . ."

"Fuck you and your white flag," Cooper said, and shot the man in the head.

Cooper turned to face Locke. "I didn't think you'd do it," he said.

"Do what?"

"Shoot that man under a white flag."

"Better that than die," Locke said. "I'm no fool, Coop."

"Obviously not," Cooper said. "It was your idea to just start shootin' into the horses. A damn good idea, too."

"I figured they wouldn't expect it," Locke said. "I thought with them standing among all these horses, something had to happen. That's a lot of horseflesh to be around when they're flailing away in a panic."

"Looks like they did most of our work for us," Cooper said.

"You did the rest," Locke said. "Shot that man when he had his hands in the air, and that one in cold blood while he was lying on the ground. You've changed a lot more than I ever thought a man could, Coop."

"So have you, John," Coop said. "There was a time you never would have shot a man under a white flag."

"He made the first move," Locke said. "He panicked and drew, because he thought we were going to kill him."

"I was," Cooper said. "Would you have shot him if he hadn't gone for his gun?"

"I guess we'll never know."

Cooper looked around at the dead men and horses. "I suppose you want to bury them?"

"No," Locke said. "I guess they got what was coming to them."

The ex-marshal looked up at the sky and said, "Guess there's no point in movin' on, then. Might as well camp here and get goin' in the mornin'—if you don't mind campin' near all these bodies."

"We'll be gone before they start to stink," Locke said. "But get going where, Coop?"

Cooper looked at him and said, "I guess we can decide that in the mornin', can't we, John?"

"I suppose we can."

SIXTY

As it turned out, it didn't do them much good to camp for the night, because neither man slept much. Locke was sad that he so distrusted Cooper that he couldn't close his eyes. The man had changed that much, was no longer the man he knew.

In the morning, the sun came up, and they had some coffee before they decided where they were going. Mostly, the sun was still behind the clouds, so they had no way of knowing if there were any gold coins still at the bottom of the Devil's Basin.

"You might have left a few," Cooper said, looking down at the water. "We have time to—"

"I'm not going in there again," Locke said. He could still feel the chill to his bones. "You can, if you want."

"I'd drown."

"If you waited long enough, you could probably wade out there."

Cooper looked at him. "You'd like that, wouldn't you?" he asked. "Get the drop on me while I'm knee-deep in water?"

"Why would I want to do that, Coop?"

The other man didn't answer, just kept looking down at the water. "Somebody'll come along and think they got real lucky when it's all dried out," he said.

"They'll never know how many men died up here for the gold, will they?" Locke asked.

"No," Cooper said. "They won't."

"Will we, Coop?"

No answer.

"Will we know how many men died?"

Still no answer.

"Seven? Or eight?"

Cooper turned his head to look at him. "You think I'd kill you for this gold, John?"

"If I didn't," Locke said, "I would have got some sleep last night."

"Would you kill me for it?" Cooper asked.

"No," Locke said. "But I'm not going to let you have this gold, and since you'd kill me for it, I guess I'd have to kill you to keep you from killing me."

Cooper took off his hat and scratched his head.

"That sounds mighty confusin' to me, John," he said. "Why don't we just split the gold? You can even take your half to the mine. At least that way, we both stay alive, and the miners get some of their money."

"Coop," Locke said, "I'll bet even if we did that, you'd double back here and wade out there to see if I left any coins."

"Wouldn't you?"

"No."

"Well," Cooper said, "I guess that's the difference between you and me, John."

"No," Locke said. "The difference between us goes much deeper than that, Coop—much deeper."

Cooper turned and walked back to the fire. He dumped the remnants of his coffee onto it, then poured the last of the pot over it, extinguishing it. Locke had his coffee cup in his left hand, so he simply stood there, holding it.

"John, I'm getting on that buckboard and leavin' with the gold," Cooper said. "There are a few loose horses up here, and you'll probably find one of them. You'll be fine."

"I can't let you do that, Coop."

"You're gonna have to kill me to stop me," Cooper said. "I don't think you'll do that."

"I'll shoot you in the leg," Locke said. "That'll stop you."

Cooper put the coffee pot down on the ground and turned to face Locke. "You ain't gonna let this go, are ya?"

"No," Locke said.

"Why do you care if these miners get paid or not?" Cooper asked. "Or if Molly Shillstone goes out of business?"

"I don't."

"You know, she was workin' with the sheriff to steal this gold," Cooper said, "only I made him a better deal."

"You could afford to make him a better deal," Locke said. "You never intended to pay him. I don't care about the miners, Coop, or the sheriff, or Molly. I care about me."

"This 'cause I fooled you?" Cooper asked. "Used you? This about your ego, John?"

"This is about friendship, Coop," Locke said. "I came all this way to help you because I thought we were friends—but the Dale Cooper I knew, he died a long time ago. So, if you draw on me, force me to kill you, I won't really be killing him, will I?"

"You'll be killin' me, John," Cooper said. "Me. I'm Dale Cooper. I'm the only Dale Cooper I can be at my age. And if I can't be who I want to be, I guess I don't care if I live or die."

"Stop talking, Coop," Locke said.

"You're right," Cooper said. "The time for talk is over."

Cooper kicked the coffee pot toward Locke and drew his gun. Locke ignored the pot, and although Cooper had outdrawn him, the ex-marshal's first shot went wide because he rushed it. It wasn't the fastest one who won, Locke knew from experience—maybe he even learned it from Cooper—but the one whose first shot flew true.

And his did.

SIXTY-ONE

John Locke drove the buckboard with the mismatched team into the Shillstone Mining camp to the cheers of the miners, who knew why he was there. They crowded around him when he halted the team in front of a shack that had a handwritten sign above the door that said "Shillstone Mining."

"Mister," a man said, grabbing his hand, "we been waitin' a long time for you."

"Are you the foreman up here?" Locke asked.

"I'm the manager," the man said. "Name's Sam Allanson."

Allanson was a barrel-chested man in his fifties, and the dirt on his hands told Locke that he got down into the mines with his men and didn't manage the operation from a chair.

"Well, Mr. Allanson," Locke said, "I got your whole payroll here, maybe minus a few coins."

"A few coins?" the man asked with a frown.

"Yeah," Locke said. "I'll explain it to you. Meanwhile, I need a few men for a burial detail."

"Burial?"

"I got a dead man in the back of the buckboard."

Locke threw the tarp off the crates and off the body of Dale Cooper. The miners crowded around, to get a look at either the body or the gold.

"Who is that?" Allanson asked.

"His name's Dale Cooper," Locke said. "Used to be a marshal a few years back."

"Yeah," the manager said. "Yeah, I heard of him. Didn't know Mrs. Shillstone had hired him to deliver the gold."

"Yeah, it was his job to deliver the payroll up here. He called me in to help him. We got hit a few different times by different groups of men bringing the gold up here, and the second time, he caught a bullet." Locke turned and looked at the assembled miners. "He died so you fellas could have your pay."

The men shuffled their feet and looked around.

"Mister," one of them finally said, "we really appreciate what you and your friend did, and we're sorry he's dead."

"We'll give him a real nice send-off, if you like," Allanson told Locke. "Won't we, boys?"

The miners whooped and hollered their agreement.

"I'd like that a lot, boys," Locke said. "And I guess the marshal would, too."

At least, the old Marshal Cooper would, he thought.

*   *   *

On the way back down the mountain to the town of Turnback Creek, Locke stopped the buckboard and retrieved the body of Sheriff Mike Hammet. Some critters had gotten to it, but it was still largely intact, and he wanted to bring it back to town. He also had recovered the man's badge from the pocket of Hoke Benson.

However, he had no intention of hiding the sheriff's part in trying to steal the gold, the way he had hidden Dale Cooper's. He had nothing to gain by keeping it a secret, and he still had some unfinished business to take care of with Molly Shillstone that the sheriff might help him with, even in death.

When he reentered Turnback Creek, he drove the buckboard directly to the office of Shillstone Mining. He set the brake and dropped down, went to the door, and knocked.

"Come in!" a man called out.

He entered, and George Crowell looked up at him from the desk. He studied the man's face intently, to see if it would betray surprise at seeing him. It did not. Apparently, Crowell had fully expected Locke to return from the mountain.

"Mr. Locke," he said. "Delighted to see you." Crowell rushed out from behind the desk to shake Locke's hand. "I assume, since you are here, that the payroll was delivered safely?"

"Safely, Mr. Crowell," Locke said, handing him a slip of paper that had been signed by Sam Allanson, "but not without incident. Marshal Cooper is dead."

"Oh, no!" Crowell said, looking aghast. "How did it happen?"

He explained how they'd been jumped several times by men interested in the gold. He lumped in the two men who had tried to kill him, just for the sake of simplicity. Then he told how they'd had a shoot-out with the seven men up at the Devil's Basin. "They were little more than gold-hungry store clerks, and they all ended up dead."

"The Devil's Basin?" Crowell asked. "What were you doing all the way over there?" Crowell continued to look concerned.

Locke realized he'd made an error in mentioning the basin. Now he had to cover it.

"We took a wrong turn, but that's where we ran into the seven men," he went on quickly, before Crowell could ask any more questions. "I believe they had been planning it for some time. They had an expert tracker with them. And I wouldn't be all that surprised if these were the same men who grabbed the first payroll."

"And what happened to those men?"

"They're all dead," Locke said. "It was during a gun battle with them that the marshal was also killed."

"How terrible," Crowell said. "Did you bring his body back to be buried, or did you bury him on the mountain?"

"I took his body to the mine with me, and they were kind enough to bury him there."

"They're a good bunch of men," Crowell said. "This dispute between them and Molly . . . it could have been—"

"Avoided?"

"Yes," Crowell said with a frown. "Avoided. It's almost as if—"

"Almost as if what, George?"

Crowell didn't answer.

"Almost as if she didn't want to settle with them?"

Crowell looked guilty for a moment, and Locke knew that was what he was thinking. But then, like a man in love, he rushed to her defense. "That would be crazy," he said. "Without a settlement, she could have lost the mine."

"Tell me something, George," Locke said. "The money she sent up there in gold? Was that the last money she could have gotten her hands on if things hadn't been settled?"

"Well," Crowell said slowly, "it was the last of the company's operating capital."

"Why would she put that much money at risk on this mountain?" Locke asked.

"Well . . . I'm not sure. She told me the miners demanded the payment in gold."

"See," Locke said, "that's what I find odd, George. Sam Allanson was surprised at two things when I delivered the payroll. First was that there was so much money."

"She told me the miners wanted to be paid in advance."

"And second, he was surprised that the payroll was in gold."

Now Crowell looked confused. "But . . . she said that was their idea."

"Where is Molly, by the way? We have some business to finish—that is, unless you can pay me?"

"Certainly," Crowell said, still confused. "Certainly, I can pay you. What was the amount again?"

"Five hundred dollars . . . each."

"Yes," Crowell said. "You'll want to collect for the marshal as well. I can take care of that."

Crowell walked back around behind the desk and knelt in front of a small safe, started to turn the dial. At that moment, the door opened, and Molly Shillstone walked in.

"George, there's a buckboard out front. Who's . . . Locke!" She reared back and stared at him in obvious shock. Crowell was still crouched over the safe, so she was able to recover her composure before he could see her.

"Surprised to see me, Molly?" he asked.

"Surprised to see you . . . today," she said, recovering nicely. "Get the payroll delivered already?"

"Safe and sound into the hands of the miners," Locke said. "Or isn't that what you want to hear?"

She walked to the desk, turned, and looked at him. "What do you mean?"

"I'll explain," he said, "after I get paid."

She looked at Crowell, who was taking money out of the safe. "Is that what you're doing, George? Paying him?"

"That's right," Crowell said. "Only the marshal got killed delivering the payroll."

"Did he?" She looked back at Locke. "I'm sorry to hear that."

"Yes," Locke said. "I'm sure you are."

"Here you go, Mr. Locke," Crowell said, approaching him and handing him the money. "One thousand dollars."

"A thousand?" Molly asked.

"Yes," Crowell said. "I'm sure Mr. Locke will give the marshal's share to his family."

"I understood the marshal had no family," she said.

"I was the closest thing," Locke said, pocketing the money. "You don't have a problem with that, do you, Molly?"

"Well, I really don't see why the marshal should get paid . . . I mean, if he's dead."

"Molly!" Crowell said.

"Was that why you hired him?" Locke asked.

"I'm sorry?"

"You hired Cooper because he had no family? Wouldn't be missed if he got killed trying to deliver your gold?"

"What are you talking about?" she asked.

"Yes," Crowell asked. "What are you talking about, Mr. Locke?"

"She never intended for the second payroll to be delivered, George," Locke explained. "She got the sheriff to agree to steal it from Cooper for her—only she didn't know I'd be along."

"That's ridiculous."

"Is it?" Locke took the sheriff's badge from his pocket and flicked it into the air. It sailed across the room and landed on the desk.

"You're saying the sheriff tried to steal the gold from you and Marshal Cooper?" Crowell asked. "And you killed him?"

"That's what I'm saying."

"And that he was working for Molly?"

"With Molly," Locke said. "I think the sheriff thought he was working with Molly, not for her." He didn't mention that Cooper had turned the sheriff with the promise of a bigger cut, then killed the man after Hammet helped him get away from Locke.

"This is preposterous," Crowell said. "Why would Molly want to steal her own payroll?"

"To get out from under, George," Locke said. "Out from under her father, the mine—heck, maybe even you. Remember, the miners had no idea she was sending extra money up there or that it was in gold."

"You're crazy," Molly said.

"Why would she lie about that?" Crowell asked. "I was bound to find out sooner or later that the miners didn't request those things."

"And by that time, she would have been gone, maybe to Mexico or maybe Canada, since we're closer to there. Either way, gold would spend just as well."

"I don't believe you," Crowell said.

"I don't care whether you believe me or not," Locke said. "I wanted to get paid and wanted to let you know what was going on." He looked at Molly. "And I wanted you to know that I know. That's all. What happens after this is up to you two."

Locke turned and walked out. He went to the buckboard, flung the tarp off, picked up the sheriff's body, and walked back into the office with it slung over his shoulder. Crowell and Molly were facing off, and it looked as if she was trying to explain something to him.

"—Lot of explaining to do, Molly," Crowell was saying. "I've been worried about you for some time, but this—"

"—You know me better than that, George," she was

saying, trying to talk over him. "I wouldn't do that to you. I love—"

"Excuse me," Locke said. He split them and dropped the dead sheriff onto the desk, right on top of the badge. "I believe this is yours."

He left again, this time closing the door behind him, and went to buy a horse.

When Locke rode out of Turnback Creek, he had no idea how things had turned out between Crowell and Molly. He actually didn't care what happened to the Shillstone mine. The miners had been paid, several months in advance. If the mine closed down, they'd be taken care of for a while.

Had the mine shown signs of drying up? Was that why Molly was planning to run off with the last of Shillstone Mining's operating capital? Run out on the bank notes?

He was a mile outside Turnback Creek when he stopped thinking about any of them at all. His thoughts at that point were for Dale Cooper. He was saddened by what had happened to the man, and he was angry at Cooper for forcing his hand and making him kill him. It seemed to him that when the man died, so did all the good memories of him.

He was two miles out of town when he stopped thinking about Dale Cooper.

None of the people he was leaving behind was worth more than an extra two miles of thought, anyway.

EPILOGUE

Dan Hagen came over the mountain, pulling on Henrietta's lead. He stopped short and stared down at the Devil's Basin. It was still wet, but most of the water had already drained out from the previous week's heavy rain. The bright sun reflected off about one inch of water that was left at the bottom.

"There it is, ol' girl," he said to the mule. "Bet she was chock full of water last week. Don't look like no bodies down there."

There was something down there, though. The sun was glinting off something in the shallow water.

"You gonna give me a hard time today, girl?" he asked the mule, scratching it behind the ears.

The mule shook its shaggy head and took a step forward.

"Good girl," Hagen said. "Let's get back over our mountain."

Hagen and Henrietta walked down into the basin, where they sloshed through the water that was waiting for the sun to evaporate it. This close, he could see that the sun was reflecting off small pieces of something lying at the bottom.

"What have we got here, girl?" he said. He stopped, dropped the reins to the ground, then leaned over to pick something out of the water.

"What the hell—" He stared at the gold coin lying in the palm of his hand. He bent over and picked up another one, then a third. These were already minted coins, not nuggets, so they hadn't come out of the ground.

He kept picking them up until he had a handful of them, then turned to show them to Henrietta.

"I don't know how much these are worth, girl," he said, "but somebody dropped 'em, and we found 'em, and it's definitely finder's keepers on this mountain. We're gonna eat good soon as we get to town."

He walked around and dropped the coins into one of his saddlebags, then looked around to make sure he had not missed any more.

"Looks like the basin took somethin' from somebody, girl," he said, picking up the lead again, "but for once it gave us somethin'. Yessir, it sure did give us somethin'."

ROUND 'EM UP!

THE BEST IN WESTERNS FROM POCKET STAR BOOKS

CAMERON JUDD
The Carrigan Brothers series
Shootout in Dodge City
Revenge on Shadow Trail

COTTON SMITH
The Texas Ranger series
The Thirteenth Bullet

GARY SVEE
Spur Award-winning author
The Peacemaker's Vengeance
Spirit Wolf
Showdown at Buffalo Jump
Sanctuary

JORY SHERMAN
The Owl Hoot Trail series
Abilene Gun Down

Available wherever books are sold! 10489-1

Visit
❖ **Pocket Books** ❖
online at

....

www.SimonSays.com

....

Keep up on the latest new
releases from your favorite
authors, as well as author
appearances, news, chats,
special offers and more.

SIMON & SCHUSTER
A VIACOM COMPANY
www.SimonSays.com

Pocket
Books

2381-01